Edgar Wallace was born illegitimately in 1875 in Greenwich and adopted by George Freeman, a porter at Billingsgate fish market. At eleven, Wallace sold newspapers at Ludgate Circus and on leaving school took a job with a printer. He enlisted in the Royal West Kent Regiment, later transferring to the Medical Staff Corps and was sent to South Africa. In 1898 he published a collection of poems called *The Mission that Failed*, left the army and became a correspondent for Reuters.

Wallace became the South African war correspondent for *The Daily Mail*. His articles were later published as *Unofficial Dispatches* and his outspokenness infuriated Kitchener, who banned him as a war correspondent until the First World War. He edited the *Rand Daily Mail*, but gambled disastrously on the South African Stock Market, returning to England to report on crimes and hanging trials. He became editor of *The Evening News*, then in 1905 founded the Tallis Press, publishing *Smith*, a collection of soldier stories, and *Four Just Men*. At various times he worked on *The Standard*, *The Star*, *The Week-End Racing Supplement* and *The Story Journal*.

In 1917 he became a Special Constable at Lincoln's Inn and also a special interrogator for the War Office. His first marriage to Ivy Caldecott, daughter of a missionary, had ended in divorce and he married his much younger secretary, Violet King.

The Daily Mail sent Wallace to investigate atrocities in the Belgian Congo, a trip that provided material for his *Sanders of the River* books. In 1923 he became Chairman of the Press Club and in 1931 stood as a Liberal candidate at Blackpool. On being offered a scriptwriting contract at RKO, Wallace went to Hollywood. He died in 1932, on his way to work on the screenplay for *King Kong*.

BY THE SAME AUTHOR
ALL PUBLISHED BY HOUSE OF STRATUS

BIG FOOT
THE BLACK ABBOT
BONES IN LONDON
BONES OF THE RIVER
THE CLUE OF THE TWISTED CANDLE
THE DAFFODIL MYSTERY
THE FRIGHTENED LADY
THE JOKER
SANDERS
THE SQUARE EMERALD
THE THREE JUST MEN
THE THREE OAK MYSTERY

The Man
Who Knew

HOUSE OF
STRATUS

This edition published in 2001 by House of Stratus, an imprint of Stratus Holdings plc, 24c Old Burlington Street, London, W1X 1RL, UK.

www.houseofstratus.com

Typeset, printed and bound by House of Stratus.

A catalogue record for this book is available from the British Library.

ISBN 1-84232-696-1

Contents

THE MAN IN THE LABORATORY   1

THE GIRL WHO CRIED   10

FOUR IMPORTANT CHARACTERS   17

THE ACCOUNTANT AT THE BANK   26

JOHN MINUTE'S LEGACY   33

THE MAN WHO KNEW   45

INTRODUCING MR REX HOLLAND   50

SERGEANT SMITH CALLS   63

FRANK MERRIL AT THE ALTER   73

A MURDER   83

THE CASE AGAINST FRANK MERRIL   97

THE TRIAL OF FRANK MERRIL   106

THE MAN WHO CAME TO MONTREUX   117

THE MAN WHO LOOKED LIKE FRANK   126

A LETTER IN THE GRATE   134

THE COMING OF SERGEANT SMITH   139

THE MAN CALLED "MERRIL"   152

THE MAN IN THE LABORATORY

The room was a small one and had been chosen for its remoteness from the dwelling rooms. It had formed the billiard room which the former owner of Weald Lodge had added to his premises, and John Minute, who had neither the time nor the patience for billiards, had readily handed over his damp annexe to his scientific secretary.

Along one side ran a plain deal bench, which was crowded with glass stills and test tubes. In the middle was as plain a table with half a dozen books, a microscope under a glass shade, a little wooden case which was opened to display an array of delicate scientific instruments, a Bunsen burner which was burning bluely under a small glass bowl half filled with a dark and turgid concoction.

The face of the man sitting at the table watching this unsavoury stew was hidden behind a mica and rubber mask, for the fumes which being were given off by the fluid were neither pleasant nor healthy. Save for a shaded light upon the table and the blue glow of the Bunsen lamp, the room was in darkness. Now and again the student would take a glass rod, dip it for an instant into the boiling liquid, and lifting it would allow drop by drop to fall from the rod on to the litmus paper. What he saw was evidently satisfactory, and presently he turned out the Bunsen lamp, walked to the window and opened it and switched on an electric fan to aid the process of ventilation.

He removed his mask, revealing the face of a good-looking young man, rather pale, with a slight dark moustache and heavy black wavy hair. He closed the window, filled his pipe from the well-worn pouch which he took from his pocket, and began to write in a notebook,

1

stopping now and again to consult some authority from the books before him.

In half an hour he had finished this work, had blotted and closed his book, and pushing back his chair gave himself up to reverie. They were not pleasant thoughts, to judge by his face. He pulled from his inside pocket a leather case and opened it. From this he took a photograph. It was the picture of a girl of sixteen. It was a pretty face, a little sad, but attractive in its very weakness. He looked at it for a long time, shaking his head as at an unpleasant thought.

There came a gentle rap at the door, and quickly he replaced the photograph in its case, folded it and returned it to his pocket as he rose to unlock the door.

John Minute, who entered, sniffed suspiciously.

"What beastly smells you have in here, Jasper!" he growled. "Why on earth don't they invent chemicals that are more agreeable to the nose?"

Jasper Cole laughed quietly.

"I'm afraid, sir, that Nature has ordered otherwise," he said.

"Have you finished?" asked his employer.

He looked at the still warm bowl of fluid suspiciously.

"It's all right, sir," said Jasper; "it is only noxious when it is boiling. That is why I keep the door locked."

"What is it?" asked John Minute, scowling down at the unoffending liquor.

"It is many things," said the other ruefully. "In point of fact, it is an experiment. The bowl contains one or two elements which will only mix with the others at a certain temperature, and as an experiment it is successful because I have kept the unmixable elements in suspension, even though the liquid has gone cold."

"I hope you will enjoy your dinner, even though it has gone cold," grumbled John Minute.

"I didn't hear the bell, sir," said Jasper Cole. "I'm awfully sorry if I've kept you waiting."

They were the only two present in the big cold-looking dining room, and dinner was as usual a fairly silent meal. John Minute read the newspapers, particularly that portion of them which dealt with the latest fluctuations in the stock market.

"Somebody has been buying Gwelo Deeps," he complained loudly.

Jasper looked up.

"Gwelo Deeps?" he said. "But they are the shares – "

"Yes, yes," said the other testily. "I know. They were quoted at 1s. last week; they are up to 2s. 3d. I've got five hundred thousand of them; to be exact," he corrected himself, "I've got a million of them, though half of them are not my property – I am almost tempted to sell."

"Perhaps they have found gold," suggested Jasper.

John Minute snorted.

"If there is gold in the Gwelo Deeps there are diamonds on the Downs," he added scornfully. "By the way, the other five hundred thousand shares belong to May."

Jasper Cole raised his eyebrows as much in interrogation as in surprise.

John Minute leant back in his chair and manipulated his gold toothpick.

"May Nuttall's father was the best friend I ever had," he said gruffly. "He lured me into the Gwelo Deeps against my better judgement. We sank a bore three thousand feet and found everything except gold."

He gave one of his brief rumbling chuckles.

"I wish the mine had been a success. Poor old Bill Nuttall! He helped me in some tight places."

"And I think you have done your best for his daughter, sir."

"She's a nice girl," said John Minute, "a dear girl. I'm not taken with girls" – he made a wry face – "but May is as honest and as sweet as they make them. She's the sort of girl who looks you in the eye when she talks to you – there's no damned nonsense about May."

Jasper Cole concealed a smile.

"What the devil are you grinning at?" demanded John Minute.

"I also was thinking that there was no nonsense about her," he said.

3

John Minute swung round.

"Jasper," he said, "May is the kind of girl I would like you to marry; in fact, she is the girl I would like you to marry."

"I think Frank would have something to say about that," said the other, stirring his coffee.

"Frank!" snorted John Minute. "What the devil do I care about Frank? Frank has to do as he's told. He's a lucky young man, and a bit of a rascal, too, I'm thinking. Frank would marry anybody with a pretty face. Why, if I hadn't interfered – "

Jasper looked up.

"Yes?"

"Never mind," growled John Minute.

As was his practice, he sat a long time over dinner, half awake and half asleep. Jasper had annexed one of the newspapers and was reading it. This was the routine which marked every evening of his life save on those occasions when he made a visit to London, He was in the midst of an article by a famous scientist on Radium emanation, when John Minute continued a conversation which he had broken off an hour ago.

"I'm worried about May sometimes."

Jasper put down his paper.

"Worried – why?"

"I am worried; isn't that enough?" growled the other. "I wish you wouldn't ask me a lot of questions, Jasper. You irritate me beyond endurance."

"Well, I'll take it that you're worried," said his confidential secretary patiently, "and that you've good reason."

"I feel responsible for her, and I hate responsibilities of all kinds. The responsibilities of children – "

He winced and changed the subject, nor did he return to it for several days.

Instead he opened up a new line.

"Sergeant Smith was here when I was out, I understand," he said.

"He came this afternoon – yes."

"Did you see him?"

Jasper nodded.

"What did he want?"

"He wanted to see you, as far as I could make out. You were saying the other day that he drinks?"

"Drinks!" said the other scornfully. "He doesn't drink, he eats it. What do you think about Sergeant Smith?" he demanded.

"I think he is a very curious person," said the other frankly, "and I can't understand why you go to such trouble to shield him or why you send him money every week."

"One of these days you will understand," said the other, and his prophecy was to be fulfilled. "For the present, it is enough to say that there are two ways out of a difficulty, one of which is unpleasant and one of which is less unpleasant. I take the less unpleasant of the two. It is less unpleasant to pay Sergeant Smith a weekly stipend than it is to be annoyed – and I should most certainly be annoyed if I did not pay him."

He rose up slowly from the chair and stretched himself.

"Sergeant Smith," he said again, "is a pretty tough proposition. I know, and I have known him for years. In my business, Jasper, I have had to know some queer people and I've had to do some queer things. I am not so sure that they would look well in print, though I am not sensitive as to what newspapers say about me or I should have been in my grave years ago; but Sergeant Smith and his knowledge touches me at a raw place. You are always messing about with narcotics and muck of all kinds, and you will understand when I tell you that the money I give Sergeant Smith every week serves a double purpose. It is an opiate and a prophy – "

"Prophylactic," suggested the other.

"That's the word," said John Minute. "I was never a whale at the long 'uns; when I was twelve I couldn't write my own name, and when I was nineteen I used to spell it with two n's."

He chuckled again.

"Opiate and prophylactic," he repeated, nodding his head. "That's Sergeant Smith. He is a dangerous devil because he is a rascal."

"Constable Wiseman – " began Jasper.

"Constable Wiseman," snapped John Minute, rubbing his hand through his rumpled grey hair, "is a dangerous devil because he's a fool. What has Constable Wiseman been here about?"

"He didn't come here," smiled Jasper. "I met him on the road and had a little talk with him."

"You might have been better employed," said John Minute gruffly; "that silly ass has summoned me three times. One of these days I'll get him thrown out of the force."

"He's not a bad sort of fellow," soothed Jasper Cole; "he's rather stupid, but otherwise he is a decent, well-conducted man with a sense of the law."

"Did he say anything worth repeating?" asked John Minute.

"He was saying that Sergeant Smith is a disciplinarian."

"I know of nobody more of a disciplinarian than Sergeant Smith," said the other sarcastically, "particularly when he is getting over a jag. The keenest sense of duty is that possessed by a man who has broken the law and has not been found out. I think I will go to bed," he added, looking at the clock on the mantelpiece. "I am going up to town tomorrow; I want to see May."

"Is anything worrying you?" asked Jasper.

"The bank is worrying me," said the old man.

Jasper Cole looked at him steadily.

"What's wrong with the bank?"

"There is nothing wrong with the bank, and the knowledge that my dear nephew, Frank Merril, Esq., is accountant at one of its branches, removes any lingering doubt in my mind as to its stability. And I wish to Heaven you'd get out of the habit of asking me 'why' this happens or 'why' I do that."

Jasper lit a cigar before replying.

"The only way you can find things out in this world is by asking questions."

"Well, ask somebody else," boomed John Minute at the door.

Jasper took up his paper, but was not to be left to the enjoyment its columns offered, for five minutes later John Minute appeared in the doorway, minus his tie and coat, having been surprised in the act of undressing with an idea which called for development.

"Send a cable in the morning to the manager of the Gwelo Deeps, and ask him if there is any report. By the way, you are the secretary of the Company. I suppose you know that?"

"Am I?" asked the startled Jasper.

"Frank was, and I don't suppose he has been doing the work now. You had better find out or you will be getting me into a lot of trouble with the registrar. We ought to have a board meeting."

"Am I the directors, too?" asked Jasper innocently.

"It is very likely," said John Minute. "I know I am chairman, but there has never been any need to hold a meeting. You had better find out from Frank when the last was held."

He went away, to reappear a quarter of an hour later, this time in his pyjamas.

"The mission May is running," he began, "they are probably short of money. You might inquire of their secretary. *They* will have a secretary, I'll be bound! If they want anything send it on to them."

He walked to the sideboard and mixed himself a whisky and soda.

"I've been out the last three or four times Smith has called. If he comes tomorrow, tell him I will see him when I return. Bolt the doors, and don't leave it to that jackass, Wilkins."

Jasper nodded.

"You think I am a little mad, don't you, Jasper?" asked the older man, standing by the sideboard with the glass in his hand.

"That thought has never occurred to me," said Jasper. "I think you are eccentric sometimes, and inclined to exaggerate the dangers which surround you."

The other shook his head.

"I shall die a violent death; I know it. When I was in Zululand an old witch doctor 'tossed the bones'. You have never had that experience?"

"I can't say that I have," said Jasper, with a little smile.

"You can laugh at that sort of thing, but I tell you I've got a great faith in it. Once in the King's kraal and once in Echowe it happened, and both witch doctors told me the same thing, that I'd die by violence. I didn't use to worry about it very much, but I suppose I'm growing old now, and living surrounded by the law, as it were, I am too law-abiding. A law-abiding man is one who is afraid of people who are not law-abiding, and I am getting to that stage. You laugh at me because I'm jumpy whenever I see a stranger hanging around the house, but I have got more enemies to the square yard than most people have to the county! I suppose you think I am subject to illusions and ought to be put under restraint. A rich man hasn't a very happy time," he went on, speaking half to himself and half to the young man. "I've met all sorts of people in this country, and been introduced as John Minute, the millionaire, and do you know what they say as soon as my back is turned?"

Jasper offered no suggestion.

"They say this," John Minute went on, "whether they're young or old, good, bad or indifferent – 'I wish he'd die and leave me some of his money'."

Jasper laughed softly.

"You haven't a very good opinion of humanity."

"I have no opinion of humanity," corrected his chief, "and I am going to bed."

Jasper heard his heavy feet upon the stairs and the thud of them overhead. He waited for some time, then he heard the bed creak. He closed the windows, personally inspected the fastenings of the door and went to his little office-study on the first floor.

He shut the door, took out the pocket-case and gave one glance at the portrait, and then took an unopened letter which had come that evening, and which, by his deft handling of the mail, he had been able to smuggle into his pocket without John Minute's observance.

He slit open the envelope, extracted the letter and read:

DEAR SIR,
Your esteemed favour is to hand. We have to thank you for the cheque, and we are very pleased that we have given you satisfactory service. The search has been a very long and, I am

afraid, a very expensive one to yourself, but now that discovery has been made I trust you will feel rewarded for your energies.

The note bore no heading, and was signed, "J. B. Fleming."

Jasper read it carefully, and then, striking a match, he lit the paper and watched it burn in the grate.

THE GIRL WHO CRIED

The northern express had deposited its passengers at King's Cross on time. All the station approaches were crowded with hurrying passengers. Taxi cabs and growlers were mixed in apparently inextricable confusion. There was a roaring babble of instruction and counter-instruction from policemen, from cab drivers and from excited porters. Some of the passengers hurried swiftly across the broad asphalt space and disappeared down the stairs toward the underground station. Others waited for unpunctual friends with protesting and frequent examination of their watches.

One alone seemed wholly bewildered by the noise and commotion. She was a young girl, not more than eighteen, and she struggled with two or three brown paper parcels, a hatbox and a bulky handbag. She was amongst those who expected to be met at the station, for she looked helplessly at the clock and wandered from one side of the building to the other, till at last she came to a standstill in the centre, put down all her parcels carefully, and taking a letter from a shabby little bag she opened it and read.

Evidently she saw something which she had not noticed before, for she hastily replaced the letter in the bag, scrambled together her parcels and walked swiftly out of the station. Again she came to a halt and looked round the darkened courtyard.

"Here!" snapped the voice irritably. She saw the door of a taxi cab open and came toward it timidly.

"Come in, come in, for Heaven's sake!" said the voice. She put in her parcels and stepped into the cab. The owner of the voice closed the door with a bang and the taxi moved on.

"I've been waiting here ten minutes," said the man in the cab.

"I'm so sorry, dear, but I didn't read—"

"Of course you didn't read," interrupted the other brusquely.

It was the voice of a young man not in the best of tempers, and the girl, folding her hands in her lap, prepared for the tirade which she knew was to follow her act of omission.

"You never seem to be able to do anything right," said the man. "I suppose it is your natural stupidity."

"Why couldn't you meet me inside the station?" she asked, with some show of spirit.

"I've told you a dozen times that I don't want to be seen with you," said the man brutally. "I've had enough trouble over you already. I wish to Heaven I'd never met you."

The girl could have echoed that wish, but eighteen months of bullying had cowed and all but broken her spirit.

"You are a stone around my neck," said the man bitterly. "I have to hide you away, and all the time I'm in a fret as to whether you will give me away or not. I am going to keep you under my eye now," he said; "you know a little too much about me."

"I should never say a word against you," protested the girl.

"I hope, for your sake, you don't," was the grim reply.

The conversation slackened from this moment, until the girl plucked up courage to ask where they were going.

"Wait and see," snapped the man, but added later: "You are going to a much nicer home than you have ever had in your life, and you ought to be very thankful."

"Indeed I am, dear," said the girl earnestly.

"Don't call me dear," snarled her husband.

The cab took them to Camden Town, and they descended in front of a respectable-looking house in a long dull street. It was too dark for the girl to take stock of her surroundings, and she had scarcely time to gather her parcels together before the man opened the door and pushed her in.

The cab drove off, and a motorcyclist, who all the time had been following the taxi, wheeled his machine slowly from the corner of the street where he had waited until he came opposite the house. He let down the supports of his machine, went stealthily up the steps and flashed a lamp upon the enamel ciphers over the fanlight of the door. He jotted down the number in a notebook, descended the steps again, and wheeling his machine back a little way, mounted and rode off.

Half an hour later another cab pulled up at the door and a man descended, telling the driver to wait. He mounted the steps, knocked, and, after a short delay, was admitted.

"Hullo, Crawley," said the man who had opened the door to him; "how goes it?"

"Rotten," said the newcomer; "what do you want me for?"

His was the voice of an uncultured man, but his tone was that of an equal.

"What do you think I want you for?" asked the other savagely.

He led the way to the sitting room, struck a match and lit the gas. His bag was on the floor. He picked it up, opened it and took out a flask of whisky, which he handed to the other.

"I thought you might need it," he said sarcastically.

Crawley took the flask, poured out a stiff tot and drank it at a gulp. He was a man of fifty, dark and dour. His face was lined and tanned as one who had lived for many years in a hot climate. This was true of him, for he had spent ten years of his life in the Matabeleland Mounted Police.

The young man pulled up a chair to the table.

"I've got an offer to make to you," he said.

"Is there any money in it?"

The other laughed.

"You don't suppose I should make any kind of offer to you that hadn't money in it?" he answered contemptuously.

Crawley, after a moment's hesitation, poured out another drink and gulped it down.

"I haven't had a drink today," he said apologetically.

"That is an obvious lie," said the younger man, "but now to get to business. I don't know what your game is in England, but I will tell you what mine is. I want a free hand, and I can only have a free hand if you take your daughter away out of the country."

"You want to get rid of her, eh?" asked the other, looking at him shrewdly.

The young man nodded.

"I tell you she's a millstone round my neck," he said for the second time that evening, "and I am scared of her. At any moment she may do some fool thing and ruin me."

Crawley grinned.

"For better or for worse," he quoted, and then, seeing the ugly look in the other man's face, he said: "Don't try to frighten me, Mr Brown or Jones, or whatever you call yourself, because I can't be frightened. I have had to deal with worse men than you and I'm still alive. I'll tell you right now that I'm not going out of England. I've got a big game on. What do you think of offering me?"

"A thousand pounds," said the other.

"I thought it would be something like that," said Crawley coolly. "It is a flea-bite to me. You take my tip and find another way of keeping her quiet. A clever fellow like you, who knows more about dope than any other man I have met, ought to be able to do the trick without any assistance from me. Why didn't you tell me that you knew a drug that snapped the will-power of people and made them do just as you like? That's the knockout drop to give her. Take my tip and try it."

"You won't accept my offer?" asked the other.

Crawley shook his head.

"I've got a fortune in my hand, if I work my cards right," he said. "I've managed to get a position right under the old devil's nose. I see him every day and I have got him scared. What's a thousand pounds to me? I've lost more than a thousand on one race at Lewes. No, my boy, employ the resources of science," he said flippantly; "there's no sense in being a dope merchant if you can't get the right dope for the right case."

"The less you say about my doping, the better," snarled the other man. "I was fool to take you so much into my confidence."

"Don't lose your temper," said the other, raising his hand in mock alarm. "Lord bless us, Mr Wright or Robinson, who would have thought that the nice mild-mannered young man who goes to church in Eastbourne could be such a fierce chap in London? I've often laughed seeing you walk past me as though butter wouldn't melt in your mouth, and everybody saying what a nice young man Mr So-and-so is, and I have thought, if they only knew that this sleek lad…"

"Shut up," said the other savagely. "You are getting as much of a danger as this infernal girl."

"You take things too much to heart," said the other. "Now I'll tell you what I'll do. I am not going out of England. I am going to keep my present menial job. You see, it isn't only the question of money, but I have an idea that your old man has got something up his sleeve for me, and the only way to prevent unpleasant happenings is to keep close to him."

"I have told you a dozen times he has nothing against you," said the other emphatically. "I know this business, and I have seen most of his private papers. If he could have caught you out, he would have had you long ago. I told you that the last time you called at the house and I saw you. What! Do you think John Minute would pay blackmail if he could get out of it? You are a fool, Crawley!"

"Maybe I am," said the other philosophically, "but I am not such a fool as you think me to be."

"You had better see her," said his host suddenly.

Crawley shook his head.

"A parent's feelings," he protested. "Have a sense of decency, Reginald or Horace or Hector – I always forget your London name. No," he said, "I won't accept your suggestion, but I have got a propo-sition to make to you, and it concerns a certain relative of John Minute – a nice young fellow who will one day secure the old man's swag."

"Will he?" said the other between his teeth.

They sat for two hours discussing the proposition and then Crawley rose to leave.

"I leave my final jar for the last," he said pleasantly. He had finished the contents of the flask and was in a very amiable frame of mind.

"You are in some danger, my young friend, and I, your guardian angel, have discovered it. You have a valet at one of your numerous addresses."

"A chauffeur," corrected the other; "a Swede, Jonsen."

Crawley nodded.

"I thought he was a Swede."

"Have you seen him?" asked the other quickly.

"He came down to make some inquiries in Eastbourne," said the sergeant, "and I happened to meet him. One of those talkative fellows who opens his heart to a uniform. I stopped him from going to the house, so I saved you a shock — if John Minute had been there, I mean."

The other bit his lips and his face showed concern.

"That's bad," he said; "he has been very restless and rather impertinent lately, and has been looking for another job. What did you tell him?"

"I told him to come down next Wednesday," said Crawley. "I thought you'd like to make a few arrangements in the meantime."

He held out his hand, and the young man, who did not mistake the gesture, dived into his pockets with a scowl and handed four five-pound notes into the outstretched palm.

"It will just pay my taxi," said Crawley light-heartedly.

The other went upstairs. He found the girl sitting where he had left her in her bedroom.

"Clear out of here," he said roughly; "I want the room."

Meekly she obeyed. He locked the door behind her, lifted a suitcase on to the bed and, opening it, took out a small Japanese box. From this he removed a tiny glass pestle and mortar, six little phials, a hypodermic syringe and a small spirit lamp. Then from his pocket he took a cigarette case and removed two cigarettes, which he laid

15

carefully on the dressing-table. He was busy for the greater part of an hour.

As for the girl, she spent that time in the cold dining room, huddled up in a chair, weeping softly to herself.

FOUR IMPORTANT CHARACTERS

The writer pauses here to say that the story of The Man Who Knew is an unusual story. It is reconstructed partly from the reports of a certain trial, partly from the confidential matter which has come into the writer's hands from Saul Arthur Mann and his extraordinary bureau, and partly from the private diary which May Nuttall put at the writer's disposal.

Those practised readers who begin this narrative with the weary conviction that they are merely to see the workings out of a conventional record of crime, of love and of mystery, may be urged to pursue their investigations to the end. Truth is stranger than fiction and had need to be, since most fiction is founded on truth. There is a strangeness in the story of The Man Who Knew which brings it into the category of veracious history. It cannot be said in truth that any story begins at the beginning of the first chapter, since all stories began with the creation of the world, but this present story may be said to begin when we cut into the lives of some of the characters concerned, upon the 17th day of July 19—

There was a little group of people about the prostrate figure of a man who lay upon the sidewalk in Gray Square, Bloomsbury.

The hour was eight o'clock on a warm summer evening, and that the unusual spectacle attracted only a small crowd may be explained by the fact that Gray Square is a professional quarter given up to the offices of lawyers, surveyors and corporation offices which, at eight o'clock on a summer's day, are empty of occupants. The unprofessional classes who inhabit the shabby streets impinging upon the Euston

17

Road do not include Gray Square in their itinerary when they take their evening constitutionals abroad, and even the loud children find a less depressmg environment for their games.

The grey-faced youth sprawled upon the pavement was decently dressed and was obviously of the superior servant type. He was obviously dead.

Death, which beautifies and softens the plainest, had failed to dissipate entirely the impression of meanness in the face of the stricken man. The lips were set in a little sneer, the half-closed eyes were small, the clean-shaven jaw was long and underhung, the ears were large and grotesquely prominent.

I have chosen this evening and this unhappy event as the starting point of my narrative because it happened that the appearance of this unfortunate young man attracted to Gray Square at that hour three of the more important characters in this story. One might even say four.

A constable stood by the body, waiting for the arrival of the ambulance, answering in monosyllables the questions of the curious. Ten minutes before the ambulance arrived there joined the group a man of middle age.

He wore the pepper-and-salt suit which distinguishes the country excursionist taking the day off in London. He had little side-whiskers and a heavy brown moustache. His golf cap was new and set at a somewhat rakish angle on his head. Across his waistcoat was a large and heavy chain hung at intervals with small silver medals. For all his provincial appearance his movements were decisive and suggested authority. He elbowed his way through the little crowd and met the constable's disapproving stare without faltering.

"Can I be of any help, mate?" he said, and introduced himself as Police Constable Wiseman of the Sussex Constabulary.

The London constable thawed.

"Thanks," he said, "you can help me get him into the ambulance when it comes."

"Fit?" asked the newcomer.

The policeman shook his head.

"He was seen to stagger and fall, and by the time I arrived he'd snuffed out. Heart disease, I suppose."

"Ah!" said Constable Wiseman, regarding the body with a proprietorial and professional eye, and retailed his own experiences of similar tragedies, not without pride as though he had, to some extent, the responsibility for their occurrence.

On the far side of the square a young man and a girl were walking slowly. A tall, fair, good-looking youth who might have attracted attention even in a crowd. But more likely would that attention have been focused had he been accompanied by the girl at his side, for she was by every standard beautiful. They reached the corner of Tabor Street, and it was the fixed and eager stare of a little man who stood on the corner of the street and the intensity of his gaze which first directed their attention to the tragedy on the opposite side of the square.

The little man who watched was dressed in an ill-fitting frock coat, trousers which seemed too long, since they concertina'd over his boots, and a glossy silk hat set at the back of his head.

"What a funny old thing!" said Frank Merril under his breath, and the girl smiled.

The object of their amusement turned sharply as they came abreast of him. His freckled clean-shaven face looked strangely old, and the big gold-rimmed spectacles bridged halfway down his nose added to his ludicrous appearance. He raised his eyebrows and surveyed the two young people.

"There's an accident over there," he said briefly and without any preliminary.

"Indeed," said the young man politely.

"There have been several accidents in Gray Square," said the strange old man meditatively. "There was one in 1875 when the corner house – you can see the end of it from here – collapsed and buried fourteen people, seven of whom were killed, four of whom were injured for life and three of whom escaped with minor injuries."

He said this calmly and apparently without any sense that he was acting at all unconventionally in volunteering the information, and went on: "There was another accident in 1861 on the 15th of October, a collision between two hansom cabs which resulted in the death of a driver whose name was Samuel Green. He lived at 14, Portington Mews, and had a wife and nine children."

The girl looked at the old man with a little apprehension, and Frank Merril laughed.

"You have a very good memory for these kind of things. Do you live here?" he asked.

"Oh, no!" The little man shook his head vigorously.

He was silent for a moment and then: "I think we had better go over and see what it is all about," he said with a certain gravity.

His assumption of leadership was a little staggering and Frank turned to the girl. "Do you mind?" he asked.

She shook her head and the three passed over the road to the little group just as the ambulance came jangling into the square. To Merril's surprise, the policeman greeted the little man respectfully, touching his helmet.

"I'm afraid nothing can be done, sir. He is – gone."

"Oh, yes, he's gone," said the other calmly.

He stooped down, turned back the man's coat, and slipped his hand into the inside pocket, but drew blank; the pocket was empty. With an extraordinary rapidity of movement he continued his search, and to the astonishment of Frank Merril the policeman did not deny his right. In the top left-hand pocket of the waistcoat he pulled out a crumpled slip which proved to be a newspaper cutting.

"Ah," said the little man, "an advertisement for a manservant out of this morning's *Daily Telegraph* – I saw it myself. Evidently a manservant who was on his way to interview a new employer. You see 'call at 8.30 at Holborn Viaduct Hotel.' He was taking a short cut when his illness overcame him. I know who is advertising for the valet," he added gratuitously, "he is a Mr T Burton, who is a rubber factor from Penang. Mr T Burton married the daughter of the Rev. George Smith, of Scarborough, in 1889, and has four children, one of whom is at Winchester – hum!"

He pursed his lips and looked down again at the body, then suddenly he turned to Frank Merril.

"Do you know this man?" he demanded. Frank looked at him in astonishment.

"No! Why do you ask?"

"You were looking at him as though you did," said the little man. "That is to say, you were not looking at his face. People who do not look at other people's faces under these circumstances, know them."

"Curiously enough," said Frank, with a little smile, "there is someone here I know," and he caught the eye of Constable Wiseman.

That ornament of the Sussex Constabulary touched his cap.

"I thought I recognised you, sir. I have often seen you at Weald Lodge," he said.

Further conversation was cut short as they lifted the body on to a stretcher and put it into the interior of the ambulance. The little group watched the white car disappear and the crowd of idlers began to melt away.

Constable Wiseman took a professional leave of his comrade and came back to Frank a little shyly.

"You are Mr Minute's nephew, aren't you, sir?" he asked.

"Quite right," said Frank.

"I used to see you at your uncle's place."

"Uncle's name?"

It was the little man's pert but wholly inoffensive inquiry. He seemed to ask it as a matter of course and as one who had the right to be answered without equivocation.

Frank Merril laughed.

"My uncle is Mr John Minute," he said, and added with a faint touch of sarcasm, "you probably know him."

"Oh, yes," said the other readily, "one of the original Rhodesian pioneers who received a concession from Lo Bengula and amassed a large fortune by the sale of gold mining properties which proved to be of no especial value. He was tried at Salisbury in 1897 for the murder of two Mashona chiefs and was acquitted. He amassed another fortune in Johannesburg in the boom of '97, and came to this country in 1901, settling on a small estate between Polegate and Eastbourne. He has one nephew, his heir, Frank Merril, the son of the late Dr Henry Merril, who is an accountant in the London and Western Counties Bank. He – "

Frank looked at him in undisguised amazement.

"You know my uncle?"

"Never met him in my life," said the little man brusquely. He took off his silk hat with a sweep.

"I wish you good afternoon," he said, and strode rapidly away.

The uniformed policeman turned a solemn face upon the group.

"Do you know that gentleman?" asked Frank.

The constable smiled. "Oh, yes, sir, that is Mr Mann. At the Yard we call him The Man Who Knows!"

"Is he a detective?"

The constable shook his head.

"From what I understand, sir, he does a lot of work for the Commissioner and for the Government. We have orders never to interfere with him or refuse him any information that we can give."

" 'The Man Who Knows'?" repeated Frank, with a puzzled frown. "What an extraordinary person! What does he know?" he asked suddenly.

"Everything," said the constable, comprehensively.

A little later Frank was walking slowly towards Holborn.

"You seemed to be rather depressed," smiled the girl.

"Confound that fellow!" said Frank breaking his silence. "I wonder how he comes to know all about uncle?" He shrugged his shoulders. "Well, dear, this is not a very cheery evening for you. I did not bring you out to see accidents."

"Frank," the girl said suddenly, "I seem to know that man's face, the man who was on the pavement, I mean…"

She stopped with a shudder.

"It seemed a little familiar to me," said Frank thoughtfully.

"Didn't he pass us about twenty minutes ago?"

"He may have done," said Frank, "but I have no particular recollection of it. My impression of him goes further back than this evening. Now, where could I have seen him?"

"Let's talk about something else," she said quickly. "I haven't a very long time. What am I to do about your uncle?"

He laughed.

"I hardly know what to suggest," he said. "I am very fond of Uncle John and I hate to run counter to his wishes, but I am certainly not going to allow him to take my love affairs into his hands. I wish to Heaven you had never met him."

She gave a little gesture of despair.

"It is no use wishing things like that, Frank. You see, I knew your uncle before I knew you. If it had not been for your uncle I should not have met you."

"Tell me what happened," he asked. He looked at his watch. "You had better come on to Victoria," he said, "or I shall lose my train."

He hailed a taxi cab, and on the way to the station she told him of all that had happened.

"He was very nice, as he always is, and he said nothing really which was very horrid about you. He merely said he did not want me to marry you because he did not think you'd make a suitable husband. He said that Jasper had all the qualities and most of the virtues."

Frank frowned, "Jasper is a sleek brute," he said viciously.

She laid her hand on his arm.

"Please be patient," she said. "Jasper has said nothing to me and has never been anything but most polite and kind."

"I know that variety of kindness," growled the young man. "He is one of those sly, soft-footed sneaks you can never get to the bottom of. He is worming his way into my uncle's confidence to an extraordinary extent. Why, he is more like a son to Uncle John than a beastly secretary."

"He has made himself necessary," said the girl, "and that is halfway to making yourself wealthy."

The little frown vanished from Frank's brow and he chuckled.

"That is almost an epigram," he said. "What did you tell uncle?"

"I told him that I did not think that his suggestion was possible and that I did not care for Mr Cole, nor he for me. You see, Frank, I owe your uncle John so much. I am the daughter of one of his best friends, and since dear daddy died Uncle John has looked after me. He has given me my education – my income – my everything – he has been a second father to me."

Frank nodded. "I recognise all the difficulties," he said, "and here we are at Victoria."

She stood on the platform and watched the train pull out and waved her hand in farewell, and then returned to the pretty flat in which John Minute had installed her. As she said, her life had been made very smooth for her. There was no need for her to worry about money, and she was able to devote her days to the work she loved best. The East End Provident Society, of which she was president, was wholly financed by the Rhodesian millionaire.

May had a natural aptitude for charity work. She was an indefatigable worker, and there was no better-known figure in the poor streets adjoining the West India Docks than Sister Nuttall. Frank was interested in the work without being enthusiastic. He had all the man's apprehension of infectious disease and of the inadvisability of a beautiful girl slumming without attendance, but the one visit he had made to the East End in her company had convinced him that there was no fear as to her personal safety.

He was wont to grumble that she was more interested in her work than she was in him, which was probably true, because her development had been a slow one and it could not be said that she was greatly in love with anything in the world, save her self-imposed mission.

She ate her frugal dinner and drove down to the mission headquarters off the Albert Dock Road. Three nights a week was devoted by the mission to visitation work. Many women and girls living in this area spent their days at factories in the neighbourhood, and they had only the evenings for the treatment of ailments which, in people better circumstanced, would produce the attendance of specialists. For the night work the nurses were accompanied by a volunteer male escort. May Nuttall's duties that evening carried her to Silvertown and to a network of mean streets to the east of the railway.

Her work began at dusk and was not ended until night had fallen and the stars were quivering in a hot sky.

The heat was stifling, and as she came out of the last foul dwelling she welcomed as a relief even the vitiated air of the hot night. She went back into the passageway of the house, and by the light of a paraffin lamp made her last entry in the little diary she carried.

"That makes eight we have seen, Thompson," she said to her escort. "Is there anybody else on the list?"

"Nobody else tonight, miss," said the young man, concealing a yawn.

"I'm afraid it is not very interesting for you, Thompson," said the girl sympathetically; "you haven't even the excitement of work. It must be awfully dull standing outside waiting for me."

"Bless you, miss," said the man, "I don't mind at all. If it is good enough for you to come into these streets, it is good enough for me to do the round with you."

They stood in a little courtyard, a cul-de-sac cut off at one end by a sheer wall, and as the girl put back her diary into her little net bag, a man came swiftly down from the street entrance of the court and passed her. As he did so the dim light of the lamp showed for a second his face, and her mouth formed an "O" of astonishment. She watched him until he disappeared into one of the dark doorways at the farther end of the court, and stood staring at the door as though unable to believe her eyes.

There was no mistaking the pale face and the straight figure of Jasper Cole, John Minute's secretary.

THE ACCOUNTANT AT THE BANK

DEAR FRANK

Such a remarkable thing happened last night. I was in Silver Rents about eleven o'clock, and had just finished seeing the last of my patients, when a man passed me and entered one of the houses – it was, I thought at the time, either the last or the last but one on the left. I now know that it was the last but one. There is no doubt at all in my mind that it was Mr Cole, but not only did I see his face but he carried the snakewood cane which he always affects.

I must confess I was curious enough to make inquiries, and I found that he is a frequent visitor here, but nobody quite knows why he comes. The last house is occupied by two families, very uninteresting people, and the last house but one is empty save for a room which is apparently the one Mr Cole uses. None of the people in the Rents know Mr Cole or have ever seen him. Apparently, the downstairs room in the empty house is kept locked, and a woman who lives opposite told my informant, Thompson, who you will remember as the man who always goes with me when I am slumming, that the gentleman sometimes comes, uses this room, and that he always sweeps it out for himself. It cannot be very well furnished and apparently he never stays the night there.

Isn't it very extraordinary? Please tell me what you make of it...

Frank Merril put down the letter and slowly filled his pipe. He was puzzled and found no solution either then or on his way to the office.

He was the accountant of the Piccadilly branch of the London and Western Counties Bank, and had very little time to give to outside problems. But the thought of Cole and his curious appearance in a London slum under circumstances which, to say the least, were mysterious, came between him and his work more than once.

He was entering up some transactions when he was sent for by the manager. Frank Merril, though he did not occupy a particularly imposing post in the bank, held nevertheless a very extraordinary position, and one which ensured for him more consideration than the average official receives at the hands of his superiors. His uncle was financially interested in the bank, and it was generally believed that Frank had been sent as much to watch his relative's interest as to prepare himself for the handling of the great fortune which John Minute would some day leave to his heir.

The manager nodded cheerily as Frank came in and closed the door behind him.

"Good morning, Mr Merril," said the chief. "I want to see you about Mr Holland's account. You told me he was in the other day."

Frank nodded.

"He came in in the lunch hour."

"I wish I had been in," said the manager thoughtfully. "I would like to see this gentleman."

"Is there anything wrong with his account?"

"Oh, no," said the manager with a smile. "He has a very good balance. In fact, too large a balance for his floating account. I wish you would see him and persuade him to put some of his money on deposit. The head office does not like big floating balances which may be withdrawn at any moment, and which necessitates the keeping here of a larger quantity of cash than I care to hold.

"Personally," he went on, "I do not like our method of doing business at all. Our head office being in Plymouth it is necessary by the peculiar rules of the bank that the floating balances should be so covered, and I confess that your uncle is as great a sinner as any. Look at this!"

He pushed a cheque across the table.

"Here's a bearer cheque for £60,000 which has just come in. It is to pay the remainder of the purchase price due to Consolidated Mines. Why they cannot accept the ordinary crossed cheque, Heaven knows!"

Frank looked at the sprawling signature and smiled.

"You see, uncle's got a reputation to keep up," he said good-humouredly, "one is not called 'Ready-Money Minute' for nothing."

The manager made a little grimace.

"That sort of thing may be necessary in South Africa," he said, "but here in the very heart of the money world cash payments are a form of lunacy! I do not want you to repeat this to your relative."

"I am hardly likely to do that," said Frank, "though I do think you ought to allow something for uncle's peculiar experiences in the early days of his career."

"Oh, I make every allowance," said the other, "only it is very inconvenient – but it was not to discuss your uncle's shortcomings that I brought you here."

He pulled out a pass book from a heap in front of him.

" 'Mr Rex Holland,' " he read. "He opened his account while I was on my holiday, you remember."

"I remember very well," said Frank, "and he opened it through me."

"What sort of a man is he?" asked the manager.

"I am afraid I am no good at descriptions," replied Frank, "but I should describe him as a typical young man about town, not very brainy, very few ideas outside of his own immediate world – which begins at Hyde Park Corner…"

"And ends at the Hippodrome," interrupted the manager.

"Possibly," said Frank. "He seemed a very sound, capable man in spite of a certain languid assumption of ignorance as to financial matters, and he came very well recommended. What would you like me to do?"

The manager pushed himself back in his chair, thrust his hands in his trouser pockets and looked at the ceiling for inspiration.

"Suppose you go along and see him this afternoon and ask him as a favour to put some of his money on deposit. We will pay the usual interest and all that sort of thing. You can explain that he can get the money back whenever he wants it by giving us thirty days' notice. Will you do this for me?"

"Surely," said Frank heartily. "I will see him this afternoon. What is his address? – I have forgotten."

"Albemarle Chambers, Knightsbridge," replied the manager; "he may be in town."

"And what is his balance?" asked Frank.

"Thirty-seven thousand pounds," said the other, "and as he is not buying Consolidated Mines I do not see what need he has for the money, the more so since we can always give him an overdraft on the security of his deposit. Suggest to him that he puts thirty thousand pounds with us and leaves seven thousand pounds floating. By the way, your uncle is sending his secretary here this afternoon to go into the question of his own account."

Frank looked up.

"Cole," he said quickly, "is he coming here – by Jove!"

He stood by the manager's desk and a look of amusement came into his eyes.

"I want to ask Cole something," he said slowly. "What time do you expect him?"

"About four o'clock."

"After the bank closes?"

The manager nodded.

"Uncle has a weird way of doing business," said Frank after a pause. "I suppose that means that I shall have to stay on?"

"It isn't necessary," said Mr Brandon. "You see, Mr Cole is one of our directors."

Frank checked an exclamation of surprise.

"How long has this been?" he asked.

"Since last Monday. I thought I told you. At any rate, if you have not been told by your uncle, you had better pretend to know nothing about it," said Brandon hastily.

"You may be sure I shall keep my counsel," said Frank, a little amused by the other's anxiety. "You have been very good to me, Mr Brandon, and I appreciate your kindness."

"Mr Cole is a nominee of your uncle, of course," Brandon went on with a little nod of acknowledgment for the other's thanks. "Your uncle makes a point of never sitting on boards if he can help it, and has never been represented except by his solicitor since he acquired so large an interest in the bank. As a matter of fact, I think Mr Cole is coming here as much to examine the affairs of the branch as to look after your uncle's account. Cole is a very first-class man of business, isn't he?"

Frank's answer was a grim smile.

"Excellent," he said, dryly; "he has the scientific mind grafted to a singular business capacity."

"You don't like him?"

"I have no particular reason for not liking him," said the other, "possibly I am being constitutionally uncharitable. He is not the type of man I greatly care for. He possesses all the virtues, according to uncle, spends his days and nights almost slavishly working for his employer – oh, yes, I know what you are going to say, that is a very fine quality in a young man, and honestly I agree with you, only – it doesn't seem natural! I don't suppose anybody works as hard as I, or takes as much interest in his work, yet I have no particular anxiety to carry on after business hours."

The manager rose.

"You are not even an idle apprentice," he said good-humouredly, and then: "You will see Mr Rex Holland for me?"

"Certainly," said Frank, and went back to his desk deep in thought.

It was four o'clock to the minute when Jasper Cole passed through the one open door of the bank at which the porter stood ready to close. He was well but neatly dressed and had hooked to his wrist a thin snakewood cane attached to a crook handle.

He saw Frank across the counter and smiled, displaying two rows of even white teeth.

"Hello, Jasper," said Frank, easily, extending his hand. "How is uncle?"

"He is very well indeed," replied the other; "of course, he is very worried about things, but then I think he is always worried about something or other."

"Anything in particular?" asked Frank interestedly.

Jasper shrugged his shoulders.

"You know him much better than I – you were with him longer. He is getting so horribly suspicious of people and sees a spy or an enemy in every strange face. That is usually a bad sign, but I think he has been a little overwrought lately."

He spoke easily, his voice was low and modulated with the faintest suggestion of a drawl, which was especially irritating to Frank, who secretly despised the Oxford product, though he admitted – since he was a very well-balanced and on the whole good-humoured young man – his dislike was unreasonable.

"I hear you have come to audit the accounts," said Frank, leaning on the counter and opening his gold cigarette case.

"Hardly that," drawled Jasper.

He reached out his hand and selected a cigarette.

"I just want to sort out a few things. By the way, your uncle had a letter from a friend of yours."

"Mine?"

"A Mr Rex Holland," said the other.

"He is hardly a friend of mine – in fact, he is rather an infernal nuisance," said Frank. "I went down to Knightsbridge to see him today and he was out. What has Mr Holland to say?"

"Oh, he is interested in some sort of charity and he is starting a guinea collection. I forget what the charity was."

"Why do you call him a friend of mine?" asked Frank, eyeing the other keenly.

Jasper Cole was halfway to the manager's office and turned. "A little joke," he said. "I had heard you mention the gentleman. I have no other reason for supposing he was a friend of yours."

"Oh, by the way, Cole," said Frank suddenly, "were you in town last night?"

Jasper Cole shot a swift glance at him.

"Why?"

"Were you near Victoria Docks?"

"What a question to ask!" said the other with his inscrutable smile, and turning abruptly, walked in to the waiting Mr Brandon.

Frank finished work at 5.30 that night and left Jasper Cole and a junior clerk to the congenial task of checking the securities. At nine o'clock the clerk went home leaving Jasper alone in the bank. Mr Brandon, the manager, was a bachelor and occupied a flat above the bank premises. From time to time he strode in, his big pipe in the corner of his mouth. The last of these occasions was when Jasper Cole had replaced the last ledger in Mr Minute's private safe.

"Half-past eleven," said the manager, disapprovingly, "and you have had no dinner."

"I can afford to miss a dinner," laughed the other.

"Lucky man," said the manager.

Jasper Cole came out into the street and called a passing taxi to the kerb.

"Charing Cross Station," he said.

He dismissed the cab in the station courtyard and after a while walked back to the Strand and hailed another.

"Victoria Dock Road," he said in a low voice.

JOHN MINUTE'S LEGACY

Rochefoucauld has said that prudence and love are inconsistent. May Nuttall, who had never explored the philosophies of Rochefoucauld, had nevertheless seen that quotation in the birthday book of an acquaintance and the saying had made a great impression upon her. She was twenty-one years of age, at which age girls are most impressionable and are little influenced by the workings of pure reason. They are prepared to take their philosophies ready-made, and not disinclined to accept from others certain rigid standards by which they measure their own elastic temperaments.

Frank Merril was at once a comfort and the cause of a certain half-ashamed resentment, since she was of the age which resents dependence. The woman who spends any appreciable time in the discussion with herself as to whether she does or does not love a man can only have her doubts set at rest by the discovery of somebody whom she loves better. She liked Frank, and liked him well enough to accept the little ring which marked the beginning of a new relationship which was not exactly an engagement, yet brought to her friendship a glamour which it never had before possessed. She liked him well enough to want his love. She loved him little enough to find the prospect of an early marriage alarming. That she did not understand herself was not remarkable. Twenty-one has not the experience by which the complexities of twenty-one may be straightened out and made visible.

She sat at breakfast puzzling the matter out and was a little disturbed and even distressed to find, in contrasting the men, that of the two she had a warmer and a deeper feeling for Jasper Cole. Her alarm was due to the recollection of one of Frank's warnings, almost prophetic it seemed to her now.

"That man has a fascination which I would be the last to deny. I find myself liking him, though my instinct tells me he is the worst enemy I have in the world."

If her attitude towards Frank was difficult to define, more remarkable was her attitude of mind towards Jasper Cole. There was something sinister – no, that was not the word – something "frightening" about him. He had a magnetism, an aura of personal power which seemed to paralyse the will of any who came into conflict with him. She remembered how often she had gone to the big library at Weald Lodge with the firm intention of "having it out with Jasper". Sometimes it was a question of domestic economy into which he had obtruded his views – when she was sixteen she was practically housekeeper of her adopted uncle – perhaps it was a matter of carriage arrangement. Once it had been much more serious, for after she had fixed up to go with a merry picnic party to the Downs, Jasper, in her uncle's absence and on his authority, had firmly but gently forbidden her attendance. Was it an accident that Frank Merril was one of the party, and that he was coming down from London for an afternoon's fun?

In this case, as in every other, Jasper had his way. He even convinced her that his view was right and hers was wrong. He had pooh-poohed on this occasion all suggestion that it was the presence of Frank Merril which had induced him to exercise the veto which his extraordinary position gave to him. According to his version it had been the inclusion in the party of two ladies whose names were famous in the theatrical world which had raised his delicate gorge.

May thought of this particular incident as she sat at breakfast, and with a feeling of exasperation she realised that whenever Jasper had set his foot down, he had never been short of a plausible reason for opposing her.

For one thing, however, she gave him credit. Never once had he spoken deprecatingly of Frank.

She wondered what business brought Jasper to such an unsavoury neighbourhood as that in which she had seen him. She had all a woman's curiosity without a woman's suspicions, and strangely enough she did not associate his presence in this terrible neighbourhood or his mysterious comings and goings with anything discreditable to himself. She thought it was a little eccentric in him, and wondered whether he too was running a "little mission" of his own, but dismissed that idea since she had received no confirmation of the theory from the people with whom she came into contact in that neighbourhood.

She was halfway through her breakfast when the telephone bell rang and she rose from the table and crossed to the wall. At the first word from the caller she recognised him.

"Why, uncle!" she said "Whatever are you doing in town?"

The voice of John Minute bellowed through the receiver.

"I've an important engagement. Will you lunch with me at 1.30 at the Savoy?"

He scarcely waited for her to accept the invitation before he hung up his receiver.

The Commissioner of Police replaced the book which he had taken from the shelf at the side of his desk, swung round in his chair and smiled quizzically at the perturbed and irascible visitor.

The man who sat at the other side of the desk might have been fifty-five. He was of middle height and was dressed in a somewhat violent check suit, the fit of which advertised the skill of the great tailor who had fashioned so fine a creation from so unlovely a pattern.

He wore a low collar which would have displayed a massive neck, but for the fact that a glaring purple cravat and a diamond as big as a fifty centime piece directed the observer's attention elsewhere. The face was an unusual one. Strong to a point of coarseness, a bulbous nose, the thick irregular lips, the massive chin, all spoke of the hard life which John Minute had spent. His eyes were blue and cold, his hair a thick and unruly mop of grey. At a distance he conveyed a curious illusion of refinement – nearer at hand his pink face repelled one by its crudities. He reminded the Commissioner of a piece of scene painting that pleased from the gallery and disappointed from the stalls.

"You see, Mr Minute," said Sir George suavely, "we are rather limited in our opportunities and in our powers. Personally, I should be most happy to help you, not only because it is my business to help everybody, but because you were so kind to my boy in South Africa – the letters of introduction you gave to him were most helpful."

The Commissioner's son had been on a hunting trip through Rhodesia and Barotseland, and a chance meeting at a dinner party with the Rhodesian millionaire had produced these letters.

"But," continued the official with a little gesture of despair, "Scotland Yard has its limitations. We cannot investigate the cause of intangible fears. If you are threatened we can help you, but the mere fact that you fancy there is some sort of vague danger would not justify our taking any action."

John Minute moved uncomfortably in his chair.

"What are the police for?" he asked impatiently. "I have enemies, Sir George. I took a quiet little place in the country just outside Eastbourne to get away from London, and all sorts of new people are prying round us. There was a new parson called the other day for a subscription for some Boy Scout movement or other. He has been hanging round my place for a month and lives at a cottage near Polegate. Why should he have come to Eastbourne?"

"On a holiday trip?" suggested the Commissioner.

"Bah!" said Minute contemptuously. "There's some other reason. I've had him watched. He goes every day to visit a woman at a hotel – a confederate. They're never seen in public together. Then, there's a pedlar, one of those fellows who sell glass and repair windows, nobody knows anything about him. He doesn't do enough business to keep a fly alive. He's always hanging round Weald Lodge. Then, there's a Miss Paines, who says she's a landscape gardener, and wants to lay out the grounds in some new-fangled way. I sent her packing about her business, but she hasn't left the neighbourhood."

"Have you reported the matter to the local police?" asked the Commissioner.

Minute nodded.

"And they know nothing suspicious about them?"

"Nothing!" said Mr Minute briefly.

"Then," said the other smiling, "there is probably nothing known against them and they are quite innocent people trying to get a living. After all, Mr Minute, a man who is as rich as you are must expect to attract a number of people each trying to secure some of your wealth in a more or less legitimate way. I suspect nothing more remarkable than this has happened."

He leant back in his chair, his hands clasped, a sudden thoughtful frown on his face.

"I hate to suggest that anybody knows any more than we; but as you are so worried, I will put you in touch with a man who will probably relieve your anxiety."

Minute looked up.

"A police officer?" he asked.

Sir George shook his head.

"No, this is a private detective. He can do things for you which we cannot. Have you ever heard of Saul Arthur Mann? I see you haven't. Saul Arthur Mann," said the Commissioner, "has been a good friend of ours, and possibly in recommending him to you I may be a good friend to both of you. He is The Man Who Knows."

"The Man Who Knows," repeated Mr Minute dubiously; "what does he know?"

"I'll show you," said the Commissioner. He went to the telephone, gave a number, and whilst he was waiting for the call to be put through he asked: "What is the name of your Boy Scout parson?"

"The Rev. Lincoln Lock," replied Mr Minute.

"I suppose you don't know the name of your glass pedlar?"

Minute shook his head.

"They call him 'Waxy' in the village," he said.

"And the lady's name is Miss Paines, I think?" asked the Commissioner, jotting down the names as he repeated them. "Well, we shall – Hello! Is that Saul Arthur Mann? This is Sir George Fuller. Put me through, will you?"

He waited a second, and then: "Is that you, Mr Mann? I want to ask you something. Will you note these three names? The Rev. Vincent Lock, a peddling glazier who is known as 'Waxy', and a Miss Paines. Have you got them? I wish you would let me know something about them."

Mr Minute rose.

"Perhaps you'll let me know, Sir George – " he began, holding out his hand.

"Don't go yet," replied the Commissioner, waving him to his chair again. "You will obtain all the information you want in a few minutes."

"But surely he must make inquiries," said the other, surprised.

Sir George shook his head.

"The curious thing about Saul Arthur Mann is that he never has to make inquiries. That is why he is called 'The Man Who Knows'. He is one of the most remarkable people in the world of criminal investigation," he went on. "We tried to induce him to come to Scotland Yard. I am not so sure that the Government would have paid him his price. At any rate, he saved me any embarrassment by refusing point blank."

The telephone bell rang at that moment, and Sir George lifted the receiver. He took a pencil and wrote rapidly on his pad, and when he had finished he said: "Thank you," and hung up the receiver.

"Here is your information, Mr Minute," he said. "The Rev. Vincent Lock, curate in a very poor neighbourhood near Manchester, interested in the Boy Scouts movement. His brother, George Henry Lock, has had some domestic trouble, his wife running away from him. She is now staying at the Grand Hotel, Eastbourne, and is visited every day by her brother-in-law, who is endeavouring to induce her to return home. That disposes of the reverend gentleman and his confederate. Miss Paines is a genuine landscape gardener, has been the plaintiff in two breach of promise cases, one of which came to the court. There is no doubt," the Commissioner went on, reading the paper: "...that her *modus operandi* is to get elderly gentlemen to propose marriage and then to commence her action. That disposes of

Miss Paines, and you now know why she is worrying you. Our friend Waxy has another name – Thomas Cobbler – and he has been three times convicted of larceny."

The Commissioner looked up with a grim little smile.

"I shall have something to say to our own record department for failing to trace Waxy," he said, and then resumed his reading.

"And that is everything! It disposes of our three," he said. "I will see that Waxy does not annoy you any more."

"But how the dickens," began Mr Minute – "how the dickens does this fellow find out in so short a time?"

The Commissioner shrugged his shoulders.

"He just knows," he said.

He took leave of his visitor at the door.

"If you are bothered any more," he said, "I should strongly advise you to go to Saul Arthur Mann. I don't know what your real trouble is and you haven't told me exactly why you should fear an attack of any kind. You won't have to tell Mr Mann," he said with a little twinkle in his eye.

"Why not?" asked the other suspiciously.

"Because he will know," said the Commissioner.

"The devil he will," growled John Minute, and stumped down the broad stairs on to the Embankment, a greatly mystified man. He would have gone off to seek an interview with this strange individual there and then, for his curiosity was piqued and he had also a little apprehension, one which, in his impatient way, he desired should be allayed, but he remembered that he had asked May to lunch with him and he was already five minutes late.

He found the girl in the broad vestibule waiting for him, and greeted her affectionately.

Whatever may be said of John Minute that is not wholly to his credit, it cannot be said that he lacked sincerity. There are people in Rhodesia who speak of him without love. They describe him as the greatest land thief that ever rode a Zeedersburg coach from Port Charter to Salisbury to register land that he had obtained by trickery. They tell stories of those wonderful coach drives of his with relays of twelve mules waiting every ten miles. They speak of his gambling propensities, of ten-thousand-acre farms that changed hands at the turn of a card, and there are stories that are less printable. When M'Lupi, a little Mashona chief, found gold in '92 and refused to locate the reef, it was John Minute who staked him out and lit a grass fire on his chest until he spoke.

Many of the stories are probably exaggerated, but all Rhodesia agrees that John Minute robbed impartially friend and foe. The confidant of Lo' Ben and the Company alike, he betrayed both; and on that terrible day when it was the toss of a coin whether the concession seekers would be butchered in Lo' Ben's kraal, John Minute escaped with the only available span of mules, and left his comrades to their fate.

Yet he had big generous traits and could, on occasions, be a tender and kindly friend. He had married when a young man and had taken his wife into the wilds. There was a story that she had met a handsome young trader and had eloped with him, that John Minute had chased them over three hundred miles of hostile country from Victoria Falls to Charter, from Charter to Marandalas, from Marandalas to Massikassi, and had arrived in Beira so close upon their trail that he had seen the ship which carried them to the Cape steaming down the river. He had never married again. Report said that the woman had died of malaria. A more popular version was that John Minute had followed his erring wife to Pieter Maritzburg and had shot her and had served seven years on the breakwater for his sin.

About a man who is rich, powerful and wholly unpopular, hated by the majority and feared by all, legends grow as quickly as toadstools on a marshy moor. Some were half-true, some wholly apocryphal, deliberate and malicious inventions. True or false, John Minute ignored them all, denying nothing, explaining nothing, and even refusing to take action against a Cape Town weekly which dealt with his career in a spirit of unpardonable frankness.

There was only one person in the world whom he loved more than the girl whose hand he held as they went down to the cheeriest restaurant in London.

"I have had a queer interview," he said in his gruff quick way. "I have been to see the police."

"Oh, uncle," she said reproachfully.

He jerked his shoulder impatiently.

"My dear, you don't know," he said. "I have got all sorts of people who – "

He stopped short.

"What was there remarkable in the interview?" she asked after she had ordered the lunch.

"Have you ever heard," he asked, "of Saul Arthur Mann?"

"Saul Arthur Mann," she repeated; "I seem to know that name. Mann, Mann, where have I heard it?"

"Well," said he, with that fierce and fleeting little smile which rarely lit his face for a second, "if you don't know him, he knows you, he knows everybody."

"Oh, I remember, he is The Man Who Knows!"

It was his turn to be astonished. "Where in the world have you heard of him?"

Briefly she retailed her experience, and when she came to describe the omniscient Mr Mann –

"A crank," growled Mr Minute. "I was hoping there was something in it."

"Surely, uncle, there must be something in it," said the girl seriously. "A man of the standing of the Chief Commissioner would not speak about him as Sir George did unless he had very excellent reason."

"Tell me some more about what you saw," he said. "I seem to remember the report of the inquest. The dead man was unknown and has not been identified."

She described, as well as she could remember, her meeting with the knowledgeable Mr Mann. She had to be tactful because she wished to tell the story without betraying the fact that she had been with Frank. But she might have saved herself the trouble because when she was halfway through the narrative he interrupted her.

"I gather you were not by yourself," he grumbled. "Master Frank was somewhere handy, I suppose?"

She laughed.

"I met him quite by accident," she said demurely.

"Naturally," said John Minute.

"Oh, uncle, and there was a man whom Frank knew. You probably know him, Constable Wiseman."

John Minute unfolded his serviette, stirred his soup and grunted.

"Wiseman is a stupid ass," he said briefly. "The mere fact that he was mixed up in the affair is sufficient explanation as to why the dead man remains unknown. I know Constable Wiseman very well," he said. "He has summoned me three times, once during the war for exposing lights, once for doing a little pistol shooting in the garden just as an object lesson to all tramps, and once, confound him, for a smoking chimney. Oh, yes, I know Constable Wiseman."

Apparently the thought of Constable Wiseman filled his mind through the two courses, for he did not speak until he set his fish knife and fork together and muttered something about a "silly, meddling jackass!"

He was very silent throughout the meal, his mind being divided between two subjects. Uppermost, though of least importance, was the personality of Saul Arthur Mann. Him he mentally viewed with suspicion and apprehension. It was an irritation, even to suggest that there might be secret places in his own life which could be flooded with the light of this man's knowledge, and he resolved to beard The Man Who Knew in his den that afternoon and challenge him by inference to produce all the information he had concerning his past

There was much that was public property. It was John Minute's boast that his life was a book which might be read, but in his heart of hearts he knew of one dark place which baffled the outside world. He brought himself from the mental rehearsal of his interview to what was after all the first and more important business.

"May," he said suddenly, "have you thought any more about what I asked you?"

She made no attempt to fence with the question.

"You mean Jasper Cole?"

He nodded, and for the moment she made no reply, and sat with eyes downcast, tracing a little figure upon the tablecloth with her fingertip.

"The truth is, uncle," she said at last, "I am not keen on marriage at all just yet, and you are sufficiently acquainted with human nature to know that anything which savours of coercion will not make me predisposed toward Mr Cole."

"I suppose the real truth is," he said gruffly, "that you are in love with Frank?"

She laughed.

"That is just what the real truth is not," she said. "I like Frank very much. He is a dear, bright, sunny boy."

Mr Minute grunted.

"Oh, yes, he is," the girl went on, "but I am not in love with him – really."

"I suppose you are not influenced by the fact that he is my – heir," he said, and eyed her keenly.

She met his glance steadily.

"If you were not the nicest man I know," she smiled, "I should be very offended. Of course, I don't care whether Frank is rich or poor. You have provided too well for me for mercenary considerations to weigh with me."

John Minute grunted again.

"I am quite serious about Jasper."

"Why are you so keen on Jasper?" she asked.

He hesitated.

"I know him," he said shortly. "He has proved to me in a hundred ways that he is a reliable, decent lad. He has become almost indispensable to me," he continued with his quick little laugh, "and that Frank has never been. Oh, yes, Frank's all right in his way, but he's crazy on things which cut no ice with me. Too fond of sports, too fond of loafing," he growled.

The girl laughed again.

"I can give you a little information on one point," John Minute went on: "and it was to tell you this that I brought you here today. I am a very rich man. You know that. I have made millions and lost them, but I have still enough to satisfy my heirs. I am leaving you two hundred thousand pounds in my will."

She looked at him with a startled exclamation.

"Uncle!" she said.

He nodded.

"It is not a quarter of my fortune," he went on quickly, "but it will make you comfortable after I am gone."

He rested his elbows on the table and looked at her searchingly.

"You are an heiress," he said, "for, whatever you did, I should never change my mind. Oh – I know you will do nothing of which I should disapprove, but there is the fact. If you marry Frank you will still get your two hundred thousand, though I should bitterly regret your marriage. No, my girl," he said, more kindly than was his wont, "I only ask you this, that whatever else you do you will not make your choice until the next fortnight has expired."

With a jerk of his head John Minute summoned a waiter and paid his bill.

No more was said until he handed her into her cab on the courtyard.

"I shall be in town next week," he said.

He watched the cab disappear in the stream of traffic which flowed along the Strand, and calling another taxi he drove to the address with which the Chief Commissioner had furnished him.

THE MAN WHO KNEW

Backwell Street in the City of London contains one palatial building which at one time was the headquarters of the South American Stock Exchange, a superior bucket shop which on its failure had claimed its fifty thousand victims. The ornate gold lettering on its great plate glass window had long since been removed, and the big brass plate which announced to the passer-by that here sat the spider weaving his golden web for the multitude of flies, had been replaced by a modest oxidized scroll bearing the simple legend:

SAUL ARTHUR MANN

What Mr Mann's business was few people knew. He kept an army of clerks. He had the largest collection of file cabinets possessed by any three business houses in the City, he had an enormous postbag, and both he and his clerks kept regulation business hours. His beginnings, however, were well known.

He had been a stockbroker's clerk with a passion for collecting cuttings, mainly dealing with political, geographical and meteorological conditions obtaining in those areas wherein the great Joint Stock Companies of the earth were engaged in operations. He had gradually built up a service of correspondence all over the world.

The first news of labour trouble on a gold field came to him, and his brokers indicated his view upon the situation in that particular area by "bearing" the stock of the affected company.

If his Liverpool agents suddenly descended upon the Cotton Exchange and began buying May cotton in enormous quantities, the initiated knew that Saul Arthur Mann had been awakened from his slumbers by a telegram describing storm havoc in the cotton belt of the United States of America. When a curious blight fell upon the coffee plantations of Ceylon, a six hundred word cablegram describing the habits and characteristics of the minute insect which caused the blight reached Saul Arthur Mann at 2 o'clock in the afternoon, and by 3 o'clock the price of coffee had jumped.

When on another occasion Señor Almarez, the President of Cacura, had thrown a glass of wine in the face of his brother-in-law, Captain Vassalaro, Saul Arthur Mann had jumped into the market and beaten down all Cacura stock which were fairly high as the result of excellent crops and secure government. He "beared" them because he knew that Vassalaro was a dead shot and that the inevitable duel would deprive Cacura of the best president it had had for twenty years, and that the way would be open for the election of Sebastian Romelez, who had behind him a certain group of German financiers who desired to exploit the country in their own peculiar fashion.

He probably built up a very considerable fortune, and it is certain that he extended the range of his inquiries until the making of money by means of his curious information bureau became only a secondary consideration. He had a marvellous memory which was supplemented by his system of filing. He would go to work patiently for months and spend sums of money out of all proportion to the value of the information, to discover, for example, the reason why a district officer in some faraway spot in India had been obliged to return to England before his term of duty had ended.

His thirst for facts was insatiable; his grasp of the politics of every country in the world and his extraordinarily accurate information concerning the personality of all those who directed those policies, was the basis upon which he was able to build up theories of amazing accuracy.

A man of simple tastes who lived in a rambling old house in Streatham, his work, his hobby and his very life was his bureau. He had assisted the police times without number, and had been so fascinated by the success of this branch of his investigations that he had started a new criminal record which had been of the greatest help to the police and had piqued Scotland Yard to emulation.

John Minute descending from his cab at the door, looked up at the imposing fascia with a frown. Entering the broad vestibule he handed his card to the waiting attendant and took a seat in a well-furnished waiting room. Five minutes later he was ushered into the presence of The Man Who Knew. Mr Mann, a comical little figure at a very large writing table, jumped up and went halfway across the big room to meet his visitor. He beamed through his big spectacles as he waved John Minute to a deep armchair.

"The Chief Commissioner sent you, didn't he?" he said, pointing an accusing finger at the visitor. "I know he did, because he called me up this morning and asked me about three people who I happen to know have been bothering you. Now, what can I do for you, Mr Minute?"

John Minute stretched his legs and thrust his hands defiantly into his trouser pockets.

"You can tell me all you know about me," he said.

Saul Arthur Mann trotted back to his big table and seated himself.

"I haven't time to tell you as much," he said breezily, "but I'll give you a few outlines."

He pressed a bell at his desk, opened a big index and ran his finger down.

"Bring me 8874," he said impressively to the commissionaire who made his appearance.

To John Minute's surprise it was not a bulky dossier with which the attendant returned, but a neat little book soberly bound in grey.

"Now," said Mr Mann, wriggling himself comfortably back in his chair. "I will read a few things to you."

He held up the book.

"There are no names in this book, my friend – not a single, blessed name. Nobody knows who 8874 is except myself."

He patted the big index affectionately.

"The name is there. When I leave this office it will be behind three depths of steel; when I die it will be burnt with me."

He opened the little book again and read. He read steadily for a quarter of an hour in a monotonous sing-song voice, and John Minute slowly sat himself erect and listened with tense face and narrow eyelids to the record. He did not interrupt until the other had finished, and then: "Half of your facts are lies," he said harshly, "some of them are just common gossip, some are purely imaginary."

Saul Arthur Mann closed the book and shook his head.

"Everything here," he said, touching the book, "is true. It may not be the truth as you want it known, but it is the truth. If I thought there was a single fact in there which was not true, my *raison d'être* would be lost That is the truth, the whole truth and nothing but the truth, Mr Minute," he went on, and the good-natured little face was pink with annoyance.

"Suppose it were the truth," interrupted John Minute, "what price would you ask for that record and such documents as you say you have to prove its truth?"

The other leant back in his chair, and clasped his hands meditatively.

"How much do you think you are worth, Mr Minute?"

"You ought to know," said the other with a sneer.

Saul Arthur Mann inclined his head.

"At the present price of securities I should say about one million two hundred and seventy thousand pounds," he said, and John Minute opened his eyes in astonishment.

"Near enough," he reluctantly admitted.

"Well," the little man continued, "if you multiply that by fifty and you bring all that money into my office and place it on that table in ten thousand pound notes, you could not buy that little book or the records which support it."

He jumped up.

"I am afraid I am keeping you, Mr Minute."

"You are not keeping me," said the other roughly. "Before I go I want to know what use you are going to make of your knowledge."

The little man spread out his hands in deprecation.

"What use? You have seen the use to which I have put it. I have told you what no other living soul will know."

"How do you know I am John Minute?" asked the visitor quickly.

"Some twenty-seven photographs of you are included in the folder which contains your record, Mr Minute," said the little investigator calmly. "You see, you are quite a prominent personage – one of the two hundred and four really rich men in England. I am not likely to mistake you for anybody else, and more than this, your history is so interesting a one that, naturally, I know much more about you than I should if you had lived the dull and placid life of a city merchant."

"Tell me one thing before I go," asked Minute. "Where is the person you refer to as 'X'?"

Saul Arthur Mann smiled and inclined his head ever so slightly.

"That is a question which you have no right to ask," he said. "It is information which is available to the police or to any authorised person who wishes to get into touch with 'X'. I might add," he went on, "that there is much more I could tell you if were not that it would involve persons with whom you are acquainted."

John Minute left the bureau looking a little older, a little paler than when he had entered. He drove to his club with one thought in his mind, and that thought revolved about the identity and the whereabouts of the person referred to in the little man's record as "X".

INTRODUCING MR REX HOLLAND

Mr Rex Holland stepped out of his new car and, standing back a pace, surveyed his recent acquisition with a dispassionate eye.

"I think she will do, Feltham."

The chauffeur touched his cap and grinned.

"She did it in thirty-eight minutes, sir – not bad for a twenty mile run – half of it through London."

"Not bad," agreed Mr Holland, slowly stripping his gloves.

The car was drawn up at the entrance to the country cottage which a lavish expenditure of money had converted into a bijou palace.

He still lingered, and the chauffeur, feeling that some encouragement in conversation was called for, ventured the view that a car ought to be a good one if one spent £800 on it.

"Everything that is good costs money," said Mr Rex Holland sententiously, and then continued: "Correct me if I am mistaken, but as we came through Putney did I not see you nod to the driver of another car?"

"Yes, sir."

"When I engaged you," Mr Holland went on in his even voice, "you told me that you had just arrived from Australia and knew nobody in England – I think my advertisement made it clear that I wanted a man who fulfilled these conditions?"

"Quite right, sir – I was as much surprised as you; the driver of that car was a fellow who travelled over to the old country on the same boat as me – it's rather rum that he should have got the same kind of job."

Mr Holland smiled quietly.

"I hope his employer is not as eccentric as I and that he pays his servant on my scale."

With this shot he unlocked and passed through the door of the cottage.

Feltham drove his car to the garage which had been built at the back of the house, and once free from observation he lit his pipe and, seating himself on a box, drew from his pocket a little card which he perused with unusual care.

"One: To act as chauffeur and valet," he read. "Two: To receive £10 a week and expenses. Three: To make no friends or acquaintances. Four: Never under any circumstances to discuss my employer, his habits or his business. Five: Never under any circumstances to go farther eastward into London than is represented by a line drawn from the Marble Arch to Victoria Station. Six: Never to recognise my employer if I see him in the street in company with any other person."

The chauffeur folded the card and scratched his chin reflectively.

"Eccentricity," he said.

It was a nice, five-syllable word, and its employment was a comfort to this perturbed Australian. He cleaned his face and hands and went into the tiny kitchen to prepare his master's dinner.

Mr Holland's house was a remarkable one. It was filled with every form of labour-saving device which the ingenuity of man could devise. The furniture, if luxurious, was not in any great quantity. Vacuum tubes were to be found in every room, and by the attachment of hose and nozzle and the pressure of a switch, each room could be dusted in a few minutes. From the kitchen at the back of the cottage to the dining room ran two endless belts electrically controlled which presently carried to the table the very simple meal which his cook-chauffeur had prepared.

The remnants of the dinner were cleared away, the chauffeur dismissed to his quarters, a little one-roomed building separated from the cottage, and the switch was turned over which heated the automatic coffee percolator which stood on the sideboard.

Mr Holland sat reading, his feet resting on a chair.

He only interrupted his study long enough to draw off the coffee into a little white cup and to switch off the current.

He sat until the little silver clock on the mantel shelf struck twelve, and then he placed a card in the book to mark the place, closed it and rose leisurely.

He slid back a panel in the wall, disclosing the steel door of a safe. This he opened with a key which he selected from a bunch. From the interior of the safe he removed a cedarwood box, also locked. He threw back the lid and removed one by one three cheque books, and a pair of gloves of some thin transparent fabric. These were obviously to guard against tell-tale fingerprints.

He carefully pulled them on and buttoned them. Next he detached three cheques, one from each book, and taking a fountain pen from his pocket he began filling in the blank spaces. He wrote slowly, almost laboriously, and he wrote without a copy. There are very few forgers in the criminal records who have ever accomplished the feat of imitating a man's signature from memory. Mr Rex Holland was singularly exceptional to all precedent, for from the date to the flourishing signature these cheques might have been written and signed by John Minute.

There were the same fantastic "E's," the same stiff-tailed "Y's" – even John Minute might have been in doubt whether he wrote the "eight hundred and fifty" which appeared on one slip.

Mr Holland surveyed his handiwork without emotion.

He waited for the ink to dry before he folded the cheques and put them in his pocket. This was John Minute's way, for the millionaire never used blotting paper for some reason, probably not unconnected with an event in his earlier career. When the cheques were in his pocket, Mr Holland removed his gloves, replaced them with the cheque books in the box and the safe, locked the steel door, and drew over its front the sliding panel and went to bed.

Early the next morning he summoned his servant.

"Take the car back to town," he said. "I am going back by train. Meet me at the Holland Park tube at two o'clock – I have a little job for you which will earn you five hundred."

"That's my job, sir!" said the dazed man, when he recovered from the shock.

Frank sometimes accompanied May to the East End, and the day Mr Rex Holland returned to London he called for the girl at her flat to drive her to Canning Town.

"You can come in and drink a dish of tea," she invited.

"You're a luxurious beggar, May," he said, glancing round approvingly at the prettily furnished sitting room. "Contrast this with my humble abode in Bayswater."

"I don't know your humble abode in Bayswater," she laughed, "but why on earth you should elect to live at Bayswater, I can't imagine."

He sipped his tea with a twinkle in his eye.

"Guess what income the heir of the Minute millions enjoys?" he asked ironically. "No – I'll save you the agony of guessing. I earn £7 a week at the bank, and that is the whole of my income."

"But doesn't uncle –?" she began in surprise.

"Not a bob," replied Frank vulgarly, "not half a bob."

"But – "

"I know what you're going to say – he treats you generously. I know. He treats me justly. Between generosity and justice, give me generosity all the time. I will tell you something else. He pays Jasper Cole a thousand a year! It's very curious, isn't it?"

She leant over and patted his arm.

"Poor boy," she said sympathetically, "that doesn't make it any easier – Jasper, I mean."

Frank indulged in a little grimace and then: "By the way, I saw the mysterious Jasper this morning, coming out of Waterloo Station, looking more mysterious than ever. What particular business has he in the country?"

She shook her head and rose.

"I know as little about Jasper as you," she answered.

She turned and looked at him thoughtfully.

"Frank," she said, "I am rather worried about you and Jasper. I am worried because your uncle does not seem to take the same view of Jasper as you take. It is not a very heroic position for either of you and it is rather hateful for me."

Frank looked at her with a quizzical smile.

"Why hateful for you?"

She shook her head.

"I would like to tell you everything, but that would not be fair."

"To whom?" Frank asked quickly.

"To you, your uncle, or to Jasper."

He came nearer to her.

"Have you so warm a feeling for Jasper?" he said.

"I have no warm feeling for anybody," she said candidly. "Oh, don't look so glum, Frank. I suppose I am slow to develop, but you cannot expect me to have any very decided views yet awhile."

Frank smiled ruefully.

"That is my one big trouble, dear," he said quietly, "bigger than anything else in the world."

She stood with her hand on the door, hesitating, a look of perplexity upon her beautiful face. She was of the tall, slender type, a girl slowly ripening into womanhood. She might have been described as cold and a little repressive, but the truth was that she was as yet untouched by the fires of passion, and for all her twenty-one years she was still something of the healthy schoolgirl with a schoolgirl's impatience of sentiment.

"I am the last to spin a hard-luck yarn," Frank went on, "but I have not had the best of everything, dear. I started wrong with my uncle. He never liked my father nor any of my father's family. His treatment of his wife was infamous. My poor governor was one of those easy-going fellows who was always in trouble, and it was always John Minute's job to get him out. I don't like talking about him," he hesitated.

She nodded.

"I know," she said sympathetically.

"Father was not the rotter that Uncle John thinks he was. He had his good points. He was careless and he drank much more than was good for him, but all the scrapes he fell into were due to this latter failing."

The girl knew the story of Dr Merril. It had been sketched briefly but vividly by John Minute. She knew also some of those scrapes which had involved Dr Merril's ruin, material and moral.

"Frank," she said, "if I could help you in any way, I would do it."

"You can help me absolutely," said the young man quietly, "by marrying me."

She gasped.

"When?" she asked, startled.

"Now, next week, at any rate soon," he smiled and, crossing to her, caught her hand in his.

"May, dear, you know I love you. You know there is nothing in the world I would not do for you, no sacrifice that I would not make."

She shook her head.

"You must give me some time to think about this, Frank," she said.

"Don't go," he begged. "You cannot know how urgent is my need of you. Uncle John has told you a great deal about me, but has he told you this – that my only hope of independence – independence of his millions and his influence – you cannot know how widespread or how pernicious that influence is," he said with an unaccustomed passion in his voice, "lies in my marriage before my twenty-fourth birthday?"

"Frank!"

"It is true. I cannot tell you any more, but John Minute knows. If I am married within the next ten days," he snapped his fingers, "that for his millions. I am independent of his legacies, independent of his patronage."

She stared at him open-eyed.

"You never told me this before."

He shook his head a little despairingly.

"There are some things I can never tell you, May, and some things which you can never know till we are married. I only ask you to trust me."

"But suppose – " she faltered, "you are not married within ten days, what will happen?"

He shrugged his shoulders.

"I am John's liege man of life and limb and of earthly regard," he quoted flippantly. "I shall wait hopefully for the only release that can come, the release which his death will bring. I hate saying that, for there is something about him that I like enormously, but that is the truth, and, May," he said, still holding her hand and looking earnestly into her face, "I don't want to feel like that about John Minute. I don't want to look forward to his end. I want to meet him without any sense of dependence. I don't want to be looking all the time for decay and decrepitude, and hail each illness he may have with a feeling of pleasant anticipation. It is beastly of me to talk like this, I know; but if you were in my position, if you knew all that I know, you would understand."

The girl's mind was in a ferment. An ordinary meeting had developed so tumultuously that she had lost her command of the situation. A hundred thoughts ran riot through her mind. She felt as though she were an arbitrator, deciding between two men, of both of whom she was fond, and, even at that moment, there intruded into her mental vision a picture of Jasper Cole, with his pale, intellectual face and his grave, dark eyes.

"I must think about this," she said again. "I don't think you had better come down to the mission with me."

He nodded.

"Perhaps you're right," he said.

Gently she released her hand and left him.

For her that day was one of supreme mental perturbation. What was the extraordinary reason which compelled his marriage by his twenty-fourth birthday? She remembered how John Minute had insisted that her thoughts about marriage should be at least postponed for the next fortnight. Why had John Minute suddenly sprung this story of her legacy upon her? For the first time in her life she began to regard her uncle with suspicion.

For Frank, the day did not develop without its sensations. The Piccadilly branch of the London and Western Counties Bank occupies commodious premises, but Frank had never been granted the use of a private office. His big desk was in a corner remote from the counter, surrounded on three sides by a screen which was half glass and half teak panelling. From where he sat he could secure a view of the counter, a necessary provision, since he was occasionally called upon to identify the bearers of cheques.

He returned a little before three o'clock in the afternoon, and Mr Brandon, the manager, came hurriedly from his little sanctum at the rear of the premises and beckoned Frank into his office.

"You've taken an awful long time for lunch," he complained.

"I'm sorry," said Frank. "I met Miss Nuttall, and the time flew."

"Did you see Holland the other day?" the manager interrupted.

"I didn't see him on the day you sent me," replied Frank, "but I saw him on the following day."

"Is he a friend of your uncle's?"

"I don't think so. Why do you ask?"

The manager took up three cheques which lay on the table, and Frank examined them. One was for £850 6s. and was drawn upon the Liverpool Cotton Bank, one was for £41,150, and was drawn upon the Bank of England, and the other was for £7,999 14s. They were all signed "John Minute" and they were all made payable to "Rex Holland, Esq." and were crossed.

Now, John Minute had a very curious practice of splitting up payments so that they covered the three banking houses at which his money was deposited. The cheque for £7,999 14s. was drawn upon the London and Western Counties Bank, and that would have afforded the manager some clue even if he had not been well acquainted with John Minute's eccentricity.

"£7,999 14s. from Mr Minute's balance," said the manager, "leaves exactly £50,000."

Mr Brandon shook his head in despair at the unbusinesslike methods of his patron.

"Does he know your uncle?"

"Who?"

"Rex Holland."

Frank frowned in an effort of memory.

"I don't remember my uncle ever speaking of him, and yet, now I come to think of it, one of the first cheques he put into the bank was on my uncle's account – yes, now I remember," he exclaimed. "He opened the account on a letter of introduction which was signed by Mr Minute. I thought at the time that they had probably had business dealings together, and as uncle never encourages the discussion of bank affairs outside the bank, I have never mentioned it to him."

Again Mr Brandon shook his head in doubt.

"I must say, Mr Merril," he said, "I don't like these mysterious depositors. What is he like in appearance?"

"Rather a tall, youngish man, exquisitely dressed."

"Clean-shaven?"

"No, he has a closely trimmed black beard, though he cannot be much more than twenty-eight. In fact, when I saw him for the first time, the face was familiar to me and I had an impression of having seen him before. I think he was wearing a gold-rimmed eye-glass when he came on the first occasion, but I have never met him in the street and he hardly moves in my humble social circle." Frank smiled.

"I suppose it is all right," said the manager dubiously, "but, anyway, I'll see him tomorrow. As a precautionary measure we might get in touch with your uncle, though I know he'll raise Cain if we bother him about his account."

"He will certainly raise Cain if you get in touch with him today," smiled Frank, "for he is due to leave by the 2.20 this afternoon for Paris."

It wanted five minutes to the hour at which the bank closed when a commissionaire came through the swing door and laid a letter upon the counter, which was taken in to Mr Brandon, who came into the office immediately and crossed to where Frank sat.

"Look at this," he said.

Frank took the letter and read it. It was addressed to the manager, and ran: –

DEAR SIR,

I am leaving for Paris tonight to join my partner, Mr Minute. I shall be very glad, therefore, if you will arrange to cash the enclosed cheque.

Yours faithfully,
REX A. HOLLAND.

The "enclosed cheque" was for £55,000, and was within £5,000 of the amount standing to Mr Holland's account in the bank. There was a PS to the letter.

You will accept this, my receipt, for the sum and hand it to my messenger, Sergeant George Graylin of the Corps of Cornmissionaires, and his form of receipt will serve to indemnify you against loss in the event of mishap.

The manager walked to the counter.

'Who gave you this letter?" he asked.

"Mr Holland, sir," said the man.

"Where is Mr Holland?" asked Frank.

The sergeant shook his head.

"At his flat – my instructions were to take this letter to the bank and bring back the money."

The manager was in a quandary. It was a regular transaction and it was by no means unusual to pay out money in this way. It was only the largeness of the sum which made him hesitate. He disappeared into his office and came back with two bundles of notes which he had taken from the safe. He counted them over, placed them in a sealed envelope and received from the sergeant his receipt.

When the man had gone, Brandon wiped his forehead.

"Phew!" he said, "I don't like this way of doing business very much, and I should be very glad to be transferred back to the head office!"

The words were hardly out of his mouth when a bell rang violently. The front doors of the bank had been closed with the departure of the commissionaire, and one of the junior clerks, balancing up his day book, dropped his pen and, at a sign from his chief, walking to the door, pulled back the bolts and admitted – John Minute.

Frank stared at him in astonishment.

"Hello, uncle," he said, "I wish you had come a few moments before. I thought you were in Paris."

"The wire calling me to Paris was a fake," growled John Minute. "I wired for confirmation and discovered my Paris people had not sent me any message. I only got the wire just before the train started. I have been spending all the afternoon getting on the phone to Paris to untangle the muddle – why did you wish I was here five minutes before?"

"Because," said Frank, "we have just paid out £55,000 to your friend, Mr Holland."

"My friend?" John Minute stared from the manager to Frank and from Frank to the manager, who suddenly experienced a sinking feeling which accompanies disaster.

"What do you mean by 'my friend'?" asked John Minute. "I have never heard of the man before."

"Didn't you give Mr Holland cheques amounting to £55,000 this morning?" gasped the manager, turning pale.

"Certainly not," roared John Minute. "Why the devil should I give him cheques? I have never heard of the man."

The manager grasped the counter for support.

He explained the situation in a few halting words and led the way to his office, Frank accompanying him.

John Minute examined the cheques.

"That is my writing," he said. "I could swear to it myself, and yet I never wrote those cheques or signed them. Did you note the commissionaire's number?"

"As it happens, I jotted it down," said Frank.

By this time the manager was on the phone to the police. At seven o'clock that night the commissionaire was discovered. He had been employed, he said, by a Mr Holland, whom he described as a slimmish man, clean-shaven, and by no means answering to the description which Frank had given.

"I have lived for a long time in Australia," said the commissionaire, "and he spoke like an Australian. In fact, when I mentioned certain places I had been to, he told me he knew them."

The police further discovered that the Knightsbridge flat had been taken furnished, three months before, by Mr Rex Holland, the negotiations having been effected by letter. Mr Holland's agent had assumed responsibility for the flat, and Mr Holland's agent was easily discoverable in a clerk in the employment of a well-known firm of surveyors and auctioneers, who had also received this commission by letter.

When the police searched the flat they found only one thing which helped them in their investigations. The hall porter said that, as often as not, the flat was untenanted and only occasionally, when he was off duty, had Mr Holland put in an appearance and he only knew this from statements which had been made by other tenants.

"It comes to this," said John Minute grimly, "that nobody has seen Mr Holland but you, Frank."

Frank stiffened.

"I am not suggesting that you are in the swindle," said Minute gruffly. "As likely as not, the man you saw was not Mr Holland and it is probably the work of a gang, but I am going to find out who this man is, if I have to spend twice as much as I have lost."

The police were not encouraging.

Detective Inspector Nash from Scotland Yard, who had handled some of the biggest cases of bank swindles, held out no hope of the money being recovered.

"In theory you can get back the notes if you have their numbers," he said, "but in practice it is almost impossible to recover them, because it is quite easy to change even notes for £500, and probably you will find these in circulation in a week or two."

His speculation proved to be correct, for on the third day after the crime three of the missing notes made a curious appearance.

"Ready-Money Minute," true to his nickname, was in the habit of balancing his accounts as between bank and bank by cash payments. He had made it a practice for all his dividends to be paid in actual cash, and these were sent to the Piccadilly branch of the London and Western Counties Bank in bulk. After a payment of a very large sum on account of certain dividends accruing from his South African investments, three of the missing notes were discovered in the bank itself.

John Minute, apprised by telegram of the fact, said nothing; for the money had been paid in by his confidential secretary, Jasper Cole, and there was excellent reason why he did not desire to emphasise the fact.

SERGEANT SMITH CALLS

The big library of Weald Lodge was brilliantly lit and nobody had pulled down the blinds. So that it was possible for any man who troubled to jump the low stone wall which ran by the road and push a way through the damp shrubbery, to see all that was happening in the room.

Weald Lodge stands between Eastbourne and Wilmington, and in the winter months the curious, represented by youthful holidaymakers, are few and far between. Constable Wiseman, of the Eastbourne Constabulary, certainly was not curious. He paced his slow, moist way, and merely noted, in passing, the fact that the flood of light reflected on the little patch of lawn at the side of the house.

The hour was nine o'clock on a June evening, and officially it was only the hour of sunset, though lowering rain clouds had so darkened the world that night had closed down upon the weald, had blotted out its pleasant villages, and had hidden the green downs.

He continued to the end of his beat and met his impatient superior.

"Everything's all right, sergeant," he reported, "only old Minute's lights are blazing away and his windows are open."

"Better go and warn him," said the sergeant, pulling his push bicycle into position for mounting.

He had his foot on the treadle, but hesitated.

"I'd warn him myself – but I don't think he'd be glad to see me."

He grinned to himself, then remarked: "Something queer about Minute – eh?"

"There is indeed," agreed Constable Wiseman, heartily. His beat was a lonely one, and he was a very bored man. If, by agreement with his officer, he could induce that loquacious gentleman to talk for a quarter of an hour, so much dull time might be passed. The fact that Sergeant Smith was loquacious indicated, too, that he had been drinking and was ready to quarrel with anybody.

"Come under the shelter of that wall," said the sergeant, and pushed his machine to the protection afforded by the side wall of a house.

It is possible that the sergeant was anxious to impress upon his subordinate's mind a point of view which might be useful to himself one day.

"Minute is a dangerous old man," he said.

"Don't I know it!" said Constable Wiseman, with the recollection of sundry "reportings" and inquiries.

"You've got to remember that, Wiseman," the sergeant went on, "and by 'dangerous' I mean that he's the sort of old fellow that would ask a constable to come in to have a drink and then report him."

"Good Lord!" said the shocked Mr Wiseman, at this revelation of the blackest treachery.

Sergeant Smith nodded.

"That's the sort of man he is," he said. "I knew him years ago – at least I've seen him. I was in Matabeleland with him and I tell you there's nothing too mean for 'Ready-Money Minute' – damn him!"

"I'll bet you have had a terrible life, sergeant," encouraged Constable Wiseman.

The other laughed bitterly.

"I have," he said.

Sergeant Smith's acquaintance with Eastbourne was a short one. He had only been four years in the town, and had, so rumour ran, owed his promotion to influence. What that influence was, none could say. It had been suggested that John Minute himself had secured him his sergeant's stripes, but that was a theory which was pooh-poohed by people who knew that the sergeant had little that was good to say of his supposed patron.

Constable Wiseman, a profound thinker and a secret reader of sensational detective stories, had at one time made a report against John Minute for some technical offence, and had made it in fear and trembling, expecting his sergeant to promptly squash this attempt to persecute his patron, but, to his surprise and delight, Sergeant Smith had furthered his efforts and had helped to secure the conviction which involved a fine of 20s.

"You go on and finish your beat, constable," said the sergeant suddenly, "and I'll ride up to the old devil's house and see what's doing."

He mounted his bicycle and trundled up the hill, dismounting before Weald Lodge, and propped his bicycle against the wall. He looked for a long time toward the open French windows, and then, jumping the wall, made his way slowly across the lawn, avoiding the gravel path which would betray his presence. He got to a point opposite the window which commanded a full view of the room.

Though the window was open there was a fire in the grate. To the sergeant's satisfaction, John Minute was alone. He sat in a deep armchair in his favourite attitude, his hands pushed into his pockets, his head upon his chest. He heard the sergeant's foot upon the gravel and stood up as the rain-drenched figure appeared at the open window.

"Oh, it is you, is it?" growled John Minute. "What do you want?"

"Alone?" said the sergeant, and he spoke as one to his equal.

"Come in!"

Mr Minute's library had been furnished by the Artistic Furniture Company of Eastbourne, which had branches at Hastings, Bexhill, Brighton, and (it was claimed) at London. The furniture was of dark oak, busily carved. There was a large bookcase which half covered one wall. This was the "library", and it was filled with books of uniform binding which occupied the shelves. The books had been supplied by a great bookseller of London, and included (at Mr Minute's suggestion) *The Hundred Best Books, Books that have Helped Me, The Encyclopaedia Britannica,* and twenty bound volumes of a certain weekly periodical which shall be nameless. John Minute had no literary leanings.

The sergeant hesitated, wiped his heavy boots on the sodden mat outside the window, and walked into the room.

"You are pretty cosy, John," he said.

"What do you want?" asked Minute without enthusiasm.

"I thought I'd look you up. My constable reported your windows were open, and I felt it my duty to come along and warn you – there are thieves about, John."

"I know of one," said John Minute, looking at the other steadily. "Your constable, as you call him, is, I presume, that thick-headed jackass, Wiseman!"

"Got him first time," said the sergeant, removing his waterproof cape. "I don't often trouble you, but somehow I had a feeling I'd like to see you tonight. My constable revived old memories, John."

"Unpleasant for you, I hope," said John Minute, ungraciously.

"There's a nice little gold farm, four hundred miles north of Gwelo," said Sergeant Smith meditatively.

"And a nice little breakwater half a mile south of Cape Town," said John Minute, "where the Cape Government keep highwaymen who hold up the Salisbury coach and rob the mails."

Sergeant Smith smiled.

"You will have your little joke," he said, "but I might remind you that they have plenty of accommodation on the breakwater, John. They even take care of men who have stolen land and murdered natives."

"What do you want?" asked John Minute again.

The other grinned.

"Just a pleasant little friendly visit," he explained. "I haven't looked you up for twelve months. It is a hard life, this police work, even when you have got two or three pounds a week from a private source to add to your pay. It is nothing like the work we have in the Matabele Mounted Police, eh, John? But, lord," he said, looking into the fire thoughtfully, "when I think how I stood up in the attorney's office at

Salisbury and took my solemn oath that old John Gedding had transferred his Saibuch gold claims to you on his death-bed, when I think of the amount of perjury – me a uniformed servant of the British South African Company, and, so to speak, an official of the law – I blush for myself."

"Do you ever blush for yourself when you think of how you and your pals held up Hoffman's store, shot Hoffman and took his swag?" asked John Minute. "I'd give a lot of money to see you blush, Crawley, and now for about the fourteenth time, what do you want? If it is money, you can't have it. If it is more promotion, you are not fit to have it. If it is a word of advice – "

The other stopped him with a motion of his hand.

"I can't afford to have your advice, John," he said; "all I know is that you promised me my fair share over those Saibuch claims. It is a paying mine now. They tell me that its capital is two millions."

"You were well paid," said John Minute shortly.

"£500 isn't much for the surrender of your soul's salvation," said Sergeant Smith.

He slowly replaced his cape on his broad shoulders and walked to the window.

"Listen here, John Minute" – all the good nature had gone out of his voice and it was Trooper Henry Crawley, the lawbreaker, who spoke – "you are not going to satisfy me much longer with a few pounds a week. You have got to do the right thing by me or I am going to blow."

"Let me know when your blowing starts," said John Minute, "and I'll send you a bowl of skilly to cool."

"You're funny, but you don't amuse me," were the last words of the sergeant as he walked into the rain.

As before, he avoided the drive and jumped over the low wall on to the road, and was glad that he had done so, for a motorcar swung into the drive and pulled up before the dark doorway of the house. He was over the wall again in an instant, and crossing with swift noiseless steps in the direction of the car. He got as close as he could and listened.

Two of the voices he recognised. The third, that of a man, was a stranger. He heard this third person called "Inspector," and wondered who was the guest. His curiosity was not to be satisfied, for by the time he had reached the view place on the lawn which overlooked the library, John Minute had closed the windows and pulled down the blinds.

The visitors to Weald Lodge were three – Jasper Cole, May Nuttall, and a stout middle-aged man of slow speech but of authoritative tone. This was Inspector Nash of Scotland Yard, who was in charge of the investigations into the forgeries. Minute received them in the library. He knew the Inspector of old.

Jasper had brought May down in response to the telegraphed instructions which John Minute had sent him.

"What's the news?" he asked.

"Well, I think I have found your Mr Holland," said the Inspector.

He took a fat case from his inside pocket, opened it and extracted a snapshot photograph. It represented a big motorcar, and standing by its bonnet a little man in chauffeur's uniform.

"This is the fellow who called himself 'Rex Holland' and who sent the commissionaire on his errand. The photograph came into my possession as the result of an accident. It was discovered in the flat, and had evidently fallen out of the man's pocket. I made inquiries and found that it was taken by a small photographer in Putney, and that the man had called for the photographs about ten o'clock in the morning of that same day that he sent the commissionaire on his errand. He was probably examining them during the period of his waiting in the flat and one of them slipped to the ground. At any rate, the commissionaire has no doubt that this was the man."

"Do you seriously suggest that this fellow is Rex Holland?"

The Inspector shook his head.

"I think he is merely one of the gang," he said. "I don't believe you will ever find Rex Holland, for each of the gang took it in turn to take the part, according to the circumstances in which they found themselves. I have been unable to identify him, except that he went by the name of Feltham, and was an Australian. That was the name he gave to the photographer with whom he talked. You see, the photograph was taken in High Street, Putney. The only clue we have is that he has been seen several times on the Portsmouth Road, driving one of two cars in which was a man, who is probably the nearest approach to Rex Holland we shall get. I put my men on to make further investigations and the Haslemere police told them that it is believed that the car was the property of a gentleman who lived in a lock-up cottage some distance from Haslemere – evidently rather a swagger affair, because its owner had an electric cable and telephone wires laid on and the cottage was altered and renovated twelve months ago at a very considerable cost. I shall be able to tell you more about that tomorrow."

They spent the rest of the evening discussing the crime, and the girl was a silent listener. It was not until very late that John Minute was able to give her his undivided attention.

"I asked you to come down," he said, "because I am getting a little worried about you."

"Worried about me, uncle?" she said in surprise.

He nodded.

The two men had gone off to Jasper's study, and she was alone with her uncle.

When I lunched with you the other day at the Savoy," he said, "I spoke to you about your marriage, and I asked you to defer any action for a fortnight."

She nodded.

"I was coming down to see you on that very matter," she said. "Uncle, won't you tell me why you want me to delay my marriage for a fortnight, and why you think I am going to get married at all?"

He did not answer immediately, but paced up and down the room.

"May," he said, "you have heard a great deal about me which is not very flattering. I lived a very rough life in South Africa, and I only had one friend in the world in whom I had the slightest confidence. That friend was your father. He stood by me in my bad times. He never worried me when I was flush of money, never denied me when I was broke. Whenever he helped me, he was content with what reward I offered him. There was no 'fifty and fifty' with Bill Nuttall. He was a man who had no ambition, no avarice – the whitest man I have ever met. What I have not told you about him is this. He and I were equal partners in a mine, the Gwelo Deep. He had great faith in the mine and I had none at all. I knew it to be one of those properties you sometimes get in Rhodesia, all pocket and outcrop. Anyway, we floated a company."

He stopped and chuckled as at the amusing memory.

"The £1 shares were worth a little less than sixpence until a fortnight ago."

He looked at her with one of those swift, penetrating glances, as though he were anxious to discover her thoughts.

"A fortnight ago," he said, "I learnt from my agent in Bulawayo that a reef had been struck on an adjoining mine, and that the reef runs through our property. If that is true, you will be a rich woman in your own right, apart from the money you get from me. I cannot tell whether it is true until I have heard from the engineers, who are now examining the property, and I cannot know that for a fortnight. May, you are a dear girl," he said, and laid his hand on her arm, "and I have looked after you as though you were my own daughter. It is a happiness to me to know that you will be a very rich woman, because your father's shares was the only property you inherited from him. There is, however, one curious thing about it that I cannot understand."

He walked over to the bureau, unlocked a drawer and took out a letter.

"My agent says that he advised me that this reef existed two years ago, and wondered why I had never given him authority to bore. I have no recollection of his ever having told me anything of the sort. Now you know the position," he said, putting back the letter and closing the drawer with a bang.

"You want me to wait for a better match," said the girl.

He inclined his head.

"I don't want you to get married for a fortnight," he repeated.

May Nuttall went to bed that night full of doubt and more than a little unhappy. The story that John Minute told about her father, was it true? Was it a story invented on the spur of the moment to counter Frank's plan? She thought of Frank and his almost solemn entreaty. There had been no mistaking his earnestness or his sincerity. If he would only take her into his confidence – and yet she recognised and was surprised at the revelation, that she did not want that confidence. She wanted to help Frank very badly, and it was not the romance of the situation which appealed to her. There was a large sense of duty, something of that mother sense which every woman possesses, which tempted her to the sacrifice. Yet was it a sacrifice?

She debated that question half the night, tossing from side to side. She could not sleep, and rising before the dawn, slipped into her dressing gown and went to the window. The rain had ceased, the clouds had broken and stood in black bars against the silver light of dawn. She felt unaccountably hungry and, after a second's hesitation, she opened the door and went down the broad stairs to the hall.

To reach the kitchen she had to pass her uncle's door and she noticed that it was ajar. She thought possibly he had gone to bed and left the light on, and her hand was on the knob to investigate when she heard a voice and drew back hurriedly. It was the voice of Jasper Cole.

"I have been into the books very carefully with Mackensen, the accountant, and there seems no doubt," he said.

"You think – ?" demanded her uncle.

"I am certain," answered Jasper, in his even, passionless tone. "The fraud has been worked by Frank. He had access to the books. He was the only person who saw Rex Holland, he was the only official at the bank who could possibly falsify the entries and, at the same time, hide his trail."

The girl turned cold and for a moment swayed as though she would faint. She clutched the lintel of the door for support and waited.

"I am half inclined to your belief," said John Minute slowly; "it is awful to believe that Frank is a forger as his father was – awful!"

71

"It is pretty ghastly," said Jasper's voice, "but it is true."

The girl flung open the door and stood in the doorway.

"It is a lie!" she cried wrathfully, "a horrible lie, and you know it is a lie, Jasper!"

Without another word she turned, slamming the door behind her.

FRANK MERRIL AT THE ALTAR

Frank Merril stepped through the swing doors of the London and Western Counties Bank with a light heart and a smile in his eyes and went straight to his chief's office.

"I shall want you to let me go out this afternoon for an hour," he said.

Brandon looked up wearily. He had not been without his sleepless moments, and the strain of the forgery and the audit which followed was telling heavily upon him. He nodded a silent agreement, and Frank went back to his desk, humming a tune.

He had every reason to be happy, for in his pocket was the special licence which, for a consideration, had been granted to him, and which empowered him to marry the girl whose amazing telegram had arrived that morning while he was at breakfast. It had contained only four words: "Marry you today. – May."

He could not guess what extraordinary circumstances had induced her to take so definite a view, but he was a very contented and happy young man.

She was to arrive in London soon after twelve, and he had arranged to meet her at the station and take her to lunch. Perhaps then she would explain the reason for her action. He numbered amongst his acquaintances the rector of a suburban church who had agreed to perform the ceremony and to provide the necessary witnesses.

It was a beaming young man that met the girl, but the smile left his face when he saw how wan and haggard she was.

"Take me somewhere," she said quickly.

"Are you ill?" he asked anxiously.

She shook her head.

They had the Pall Mall Restaurant to themselves, for it was too early for the regular lunchers.

"Now tell me dear," he said, catching her hands over the table, "to what do I owe this wonderful decision?"

"I cannot tell you, Frank," she said breathlessly. "I don't want to think about it. All I know is that people have been beastly about you. I am going to do all I possibly can to make up for it."

She was a little hysterical and very much overwrought, and he decided not to press the question, though her words puzzled him.

"Where are you going to stay?" he asked.

"I am staying at the Savoy," she replied. "What am I to do?"

In as few words as possible, he told her where the ceremony was to be performed and the hour at which she must leave the hotel.

"We will take the night train for the Continent," he said.

"But your work, Frank?"

He laughed.

"Oh, blow work!" he cried hilariously. "I cannot think of work today."

At 2.15 he was waiting in the vestry for the girl's arrival, chatting with his friend the rector. He had arranged for the ceremony to be performed at 2.30, and the witnesses, a glum verger and a woman engaged in cleaning the church, sat in the pews of the empty building, waiting to earn the guinea which they had been promised.

The conversation was about nothing in particular, one of those empty purposeless exchanges of banal thought and speech, characteristic of such an occasion.

At 2.30 Frank looked at his watch and walked out of the church to the end of the road. There was no sign of the girl. At 2.45 he crossed to a providential tobacconist and telephoned to the Savoy, and was told that the lady had left half an hour before.

"She ought to be here very soon," he said to the priest. He was a little impatient, a little nervous and terribly anxious.

As the church clock struck three, the rector turned to him.

"I am afraid I cannot marry you today, Mr Merril," he said.

Frank was very pale.

"Why not?" he asked quickly. "Miss Nuttall has probably been detained by the traffic or a tyre burst. She will be here very shortly."

The minister shook his head and hung up his white surplice in the cupboard.

"The law of the land, my dear Mr Merril," he said, "does not allow weddings after three in the afternoon. You can come along tomorrow morning any time after eight."

There was a tap at the door and Frank swung round. It was not the girl, but a telegraph boy. He snatched the buff envelope from the lad's hand and tore it open. It read simply: "The wedding cannot take place," and was unsigned.

At 2.15 that afternoon May had passed through the vestibule of the hotel, and her foot was on the step of the taxi cab when a hand fell upon her arm and she turned in alarm to meet the searching eyes of Jasper Cole.

"Where are you off to in such a hurry, May?"

She flushed and drew her arm away.

"I have nothing to say to you, Jasper," she said coldly. "After your horrible charge against Frank, I never want to speak to you again."

He winced a little, then smiled.

"At least you can be civil to an old friend," he said good-humouredly, "and tell me where you are off to in such a hurry."

Should she tell him? A moment's indecision. And then she spoke.

"I am going to marry Frank Merril," she said.

He nodded.

"I thought as much. In that case, I am coming down to the church to make a scene."

He said this with a smile on his lips, but there was no mistaking the resolution which showed in the thrust of his square jaw.

"What do you mean?" she said. "Don't be absurd, Jasper. My mind is made up."

"I mean," he said quietly, "that I have Mr Minute's power of attorney to act for him, and Mr Minute happens to be your legal guardian. You are, in point of fact, my dear May, more or less of a ward and you cannot marry before you are twenty-one without your guardian's consent."

"I shall be twenty-one next week," she said defiantly.

"Then," smiled the other, "wait till next week before you marry. There is no very pressing hurry."

"You forced the situation upon me," said the girl hotly, "and I think it is very horrid of you. I am going to marry Frank today."

"Under those circumstances I must come down and forbid the marriage, and when our parson asks if there is any just cause I shall step forward to the rails, gaily flourishing the power of attorney, and not even the most hardened parson could continue in the face of that legal instrument. It is a mandamus, a caveat and all sort of horrific things."

"Why are you doing this?" she asked.

"Because I have no desire that you shall marry a man who is certainly a forger and possibly a murderer," said Jasper Cole calmly.

"I won't listen to you," she cried, and stepped into the waiting taxi cab.

Without a word Jasper followed her.

"You can't turn me out," he said, "and I know where you are going anyway, because you were giving directions to the driver when I stood behind you. You had better let me go with you. I like the suburbs."

She turned and faced him swiftly.

"And Silver Rents?" she asked.

He went a shade paler.

"What do you know about Silver Rents?" he demanded, recovering himself with an effort.

She did not reply.

The taxi cab was halfway to its destination before the girl spoke again.

"Are you serious when you say you will forbid the marriage?"

"Quite serious," he replied, "so much so that I shall bring in a policeman to witness my act."

The girl was nearly in tears.

"It is monstrous of you. Uncle wouldn't – "

"Had you not better see your uncle?" he asked.

Something told her that he would keep his word. She had a horror of scenes, and worst of all, she feared the meeting of the two men under the circumstances. Suddenly, she leant forward and tapped the window, and the taxi slowed down.

"Tell him to go back and call at the nearest telegraph office. I want to send a wire."

"If it is to Mr Frank Merril," said Jasper smoothly, "you may save yourself the trouble. I have already wired."

Frank came back to London in a pardonable fury. He drove straight to the hotel, only to learn that the girl had left again with her uncle. He looked at his watch. He had still some work to do at the bank, though he had little appetite for work.

Yet it was to the bank he went. He threw a glance over the counter to the table and chair where he had sat for so long and at which he was destined never to sit again, for as he was passing behind the counter Mr Brandon met him.

"Your uncle wishes to see you, Mr Merril," he said gravely. Frank hesitated, then walked into the office, closing the door behind him, and he noticed that Mr Brandon did not attempt to follow.

John Minute sat in the one easy chair and looked up heavily as Frank entered.

"Sit down, Frank," he said. "I have a lot of things to ask you."

"And I've one or two things to ask you, uncle," said Frank calmly.

"If it is about May, you can save yourself the trouble," said the other. "If it is about Mr Rex Holland, I can give you a little information."

Frank looked at him steadily.

"I don't quite get your meaning, sir," he said, "though I gather there is something offensive behind what you have said."

John Minute twisted round in the chair and threw one leg over its padded arm.

"Frank," he said, "I want you to be perfectly straight with me and I'll be as perfectly straight with you."

The young man made no reply.

"Certain facts have been brought to my attention, which leave no doubt in my mind as to the identity of the alleged Mr Rex Holland," said John Minute slowly. "I don't like saying this, because I have liked you, Frank, though I have sometimes stood in your way and we have not seen eye to eye together. Now, I want you to come down to Eastbourne tomorrow and have a heart to heart talk."

"What do you expect I can tell you?" asked Frank quietly.

"I want you to tell me the truth. I expect you won't," said John Minute.

A half smile played for a second upon Frank's lips.

"At any rate," he said, "you are being 'straight' with me. I don't know exactly what you are driving at, uncle, but I gather that it is something rather unpleasant, and that somewhere in the background there is hovering an accusation against me. From the fact that you have mentioned Mr Rex Holland, or the gang which went by the name, I suppose that you are suggesting that I am an accomplice of that gentleman."

"I suggest more than that," said the other quickly: "I suggest that you are Rex Holland."

Frank laughed aloud.

"It is no laughing matter," said John Minute sternly.

"From your point of view it is not," said Frank, "but from my point of view it has certain humorous aspects, and, unfortunately, I am cursed with a sense of humour. I hardly know how I can go into the matter here," he looked round, "for even if this is the time, it is certainly not the place, and I think I'll accept your invitation and come down to Weald Lodge tomorrow night. I gather that you don't want to travel down with a master criminal who might, at any moment, take your watch and chain."

"I wish you would look at this matter more seriously, Frank," said John Minute earnestly. "I want to get to the truth, and any truth which exonerates you will be very welcome to me."

Frank nodded.

"I will give you credit for that," he said. "You may expect me tomorrow. May I ask you as a personal favour that you will not discuss this matter with me in the presence of your admirable secretary? I have a feeling at the back of my mind that he is at the bottom of all this. Remember that he is as likely to know about Rex Holland as I.

"There has been an audit at the bank," Frank went on, "and I am not so stupid that I don't understand what this has meant. There has also been a certain coldness in the attitude of Brandon, and I have intercepted suspicious and meaning glances from the clerks. I shall not be surprised, therefore, if you tell me that my books are not in order. But again I would point out to you that it is just as possible for Jasper, who has access to the bank at all hours of the day and night, to have altered them, as it is for me.

"I hasten to add," he said with a smile, "that I don't accuse Jasper. He is such a machine and I cannot imagine him capable of so much initiative as to systematically forge cheques and falsify ledgers. I merely mention Jasper because I want to emphasize the injustice of putting any man under suspicion unless you have the strongest and most convincing proof of his guilt. To declare my innocence is unnecessary from my point of view – and probably from yours also – but I declare to you, Uncle John, that I know no more about this matter than you."

He stood leaning on the desk and looking down at his uncle, and John Minute, with all his experience of men and for all his suspicions, felt just a twinge of remorse. It was not to last long, however.

"I shall expect you tomorrow," he said.

Frank nodded, walked out of the room and out of the bank, and twenty-four pairs of speculative eyes followed him.

A few hours later another curious scene was being enacted, this time near the town of East Grinstead. There is a lonely stretch of road across a heath, which is called, for some reason, Ashdown Forest. A car was drawn up on a patch of turf by the side of the heath. Its owner was sitting in a little clearing out of view of the road, sipping a cup of tea which his chauffeur had made. He finished this and watched the servant take the basket.

"Come back to me when you have finished," he said.

The man touched his cap and disappeared with the package, but returned again in a few minutes.

"Sit down, Feltham," said Mr Rex Holland. "I dare say you think it was rather strange of me to give you that little commission the other day," said Mr Holland, crossing his legs and leaning back against a tree.

The chauffeur smiled uncomfortably.

"Yes sir, I did," he said shortly.

"Were you satisfied with what I gave you?" asked the man.

The chauffeur shuffled his feet uneasily.

"Quite satisfied, sir," he said.

"You seem a little *distrait*, Feltham, I mean a little upset about something. What is it?"

The man coughed in embarrassed confusion.

"Well, sir," he began, "the fact is, I don't like it."

"You don't like what? The £500 I gave you?"

"No, sir. It is not that, but it was a queer thing to ask me to do, pretend to be you and send a commissionaire to the bank for your money and then get away out of London to a quiet little hole like Bilstead."

"So you think it was queer?"

The chauffeur nodded.

"The fact is, sir," he blurted out, "I've seen the papers."

The other nodded thoughtfully.

"I presume you mean the newspapers. And what is there in the newspapers that interests you?"

Mr Holland took a gold case from his pocket, opened it languidly and selected a cigarette. He was closing it when he caught the chauffeur's eye and tossed a cigarette to him.

"Thank you, sir," said the man.

"What was it you didn't like?" asked Mr Holland again, passing a match.

"Well, sir, I've been in all sorts of queer places," said Feltham doggedly, as he puffed away at the cigarette, "but I've always managed to keep clear of anything – funny. Do you see what I mean?"

"By funny, I presume you don't mean comic," said Mr Rex Holland cheerfully. "You mean dishonest, I suppose."

"That's right, sir, and there's no doubt that I have been in a ramp – in a swindle, I mean, and it's worrying me – that bank forgery case. Why, I read my own description in the papers!"

Beads of perspiration stood upon the little man's forehead and there was a pathetical droop to his mouth.

"That is the distinction which falls to few of us," said his employer suavely. "You ought to feel highly honoured. And what are you going to do about it, Feltham?"

The man looked to left and right as though seeking some friend in need who would step forth with ready-made advice.

"The only thing I can do, sir," he said, "is to give myself up."

"And give me up, too," said the other with a little laugh. "Oh, no, my dear Feltham. Listen, I will tell you something. A few weeks ago I had a very promising valet-chauffeur just like you. He was an admirable man and he was also a foreigner. I believe he was a Swede. He came to me under exactly the same circumstances as you arrived and he received exactly the same instructions as you have received, which, unfortunately, he did not carry out to the letter. I caught him pilfering from me a few trinkets of no great value, and instead of the foolish fellow repenting he blurted out the one fact which I did not wish him to know, and incidentally, which I did not wish anybody in the world to know.

"He knew who I was. He had seen me in the West End and had discovered my identity. He even sought an interview with someone to whom it would have been inconvenient to have made known my – character. I promised to find him another job, but he had already decided upon changing, and had cut out an advertisement from a newspaper. I parted friendly with him, wished him luck, and he went off to interview his possible employer, smoking one of my cigarettes, just as you are smoking, and he threw it away, I have no doubt, just as you have thrown it away when it began to taste a little bitter.

"Look here," said the chauffeur, and scrambled to his feet, "if you try any monkey tricks with me – "

Mr Holland eyed him with interest

"If you try any monkey tricks with me," said the chauffeur thickly, "I'll – "

He pitched forward on his face and lay still.

Mr Holland waited long enough to search his pockets, and then, stepping cautiously into the road, donned the chauffeur's cap and goggles and set his car running swiftly southward.

A MURDER

Constable Wiseman lived in the bosom of his admiring family in a small cottage on the Bexhill road. That "my father was a policeman" was the proud boast of two small boys, Joffre Haig Wiseman and Loos Somme Wiseman, a boast which entitled them to no small amount of respect, because PC Wiseman was not only honoured in his own circle but throughout the village in which he dwelt.

He was, in the first place, a town policeman, as distinct from a county policeman, though he wore the badge and uniform of the Sussex Constabulary. It was felt that a town policeman had more in common with crime, had a vaster experience and was, in consequence, a more helpful adviser than a man whose duties began and ended in the patrolling of country lanes and law-abiding villages, where nothing more exciting than an occasional dog fight or a charge of poaching served to fill the hiatus of constabulary life.

Constable Wiseman was looked upon as a shrewd fellow, a man to whom might be brought the delicate problems which occasionally perplexed and confused the bucolic mind. He had settled the vexed question as to whether a policeman could or could not enter a house where a man was beating his wife, and had decided that such a trespass could only be committed if the lady involved should utter piercing cries of "Murder!"

He added significantly that the constable who was called upon must be the constable on duty and not an ornament of the force, who, by accident, was a resident in their midst. As a regular constable only made one visit to the village, and that at the prosaic hour of 1a.m., it is doubtful whether he greatly comforted the housewives concerned, though it was observed that certain notorious male offenders went about thereafter deep in thought.

The problem of the straying chicken and the egg that is laid on alien property, the point of law involved in the question as to when a servant should give notice and the date from which her notice should count – all these matters came within Constable Wiseman's purview and were solved to the satisfaction of all who brought their little obscurities for solution.

But it was in his own domestic circle that Constable Wiseman – appropriately named, as all agreed – shone with an effulgence that was almost dazzling and was a source of irritation to the male relatives on his wife's side, one of whom had, unfortunately, come within the grasp of the law over a matter of a snared rabbit and was, in consequence, predisposed to anarchy in so far as the abolition of law and order affected the police force.

Constable Wiseman sat at tea one summer evening, and about the spotless white cloth which covered the table was grouped all that Constable Wiseman might legally call his. Tea was a function and to the younger members of the family meant just tea and bread and butter. To Constable Wiseman it meant luxuries of a varied and costly nature. His taste ranged from rump steak to Yarmouth bloaters, and once he had introduced a foreign delicacy – foreign to the village who had never known before the reason for their existence – sweetbreads.

The conversation, which was well sustained by Mr Wiseman, was usually of himself, his wife being content to punctuate his auto-biography with such encouraging phrases as "Dear, dear!" "Well, whatever next!" the children doing no more than ask in a whisper for more food. This they did at regular and frequent intervals, but, because of their whispers, they were supposed to be unheard.

Constable Wiseman spoke about himself because he knew of nothing more interesting to talk about. His evening conversation usually took the form of a very full résumé of his previous day's experience. What he said to the tramp and what the tramp said to him: how Baggin, the baker, had apologised for leaving his horse and cart unattended, of how intoxicated individuals had been ejected from wayside public-houses and been advised by Mr Wiseman that they had better go home whilst they were safe. He left the impression upon his wife – and glad enough she was to have such an impression – that Eastbourne was a well-conducted town mainly as a result of PC Wiseman's ceaseless and tireless efforts. There were some times when she wondered – good soul – what would have happened to Eastbourne when a motorcar exceeding the limits dashed down upon the unsuspecting policeman, had he not, with rare presence of mind, got out of the way. She saw Eastbourne a lawless and most undesirable community bereft of the chief pillar of its law.

"So I said to him," said Constable Wiseman: " 'My lad, you had better go home while you are safe,' and he said to me: 'All right, constable.' And I said to him: 'Not so much all right; you get home.' And he went home."

"Good gracious!" said Mrs Wiseman, wondering, no doubt, whether "he" would have gone but for her husband's timely suggestion.

There had been an important crime committed a few miles from the town, and CID officers had been sent down from Scotland Yard. Constable Wiseman complained bitterly that the matter had been taken out of "our hands". He said it in a manner which left no doubt that he meant "my hands".

"What's the good of these fellows coming down?" he asked. "They don't know the ropes. They don't know anybody in the town. They have to come to us for any information they want. Now if that matter had been put in my hands I should have gone straight off to Polegate, and I should have asked the landlord of the Red Cow if he had seen any suspicious characters passing through the village. 'Yes,' he'd have said, 'a red-nosed man and a man with a limp.' 'Which way did they go?' I'd have said. 'Through the town,' he'd have said. I should have followed them through the town, keeping my eye open for footprints, and I bet you I'd have got them! But what do these CID men do? They just loaf around the pubs. They stay at the hotels wasting the country's money. They get a clue and lose it as soon as they have got it. I never had a clue yet that I never followed to the bitter end. You remember when Raggett's orchard was robbed. Who found the thieves?"

"You did, of course, I'm sure you did," said Mrs Wiseman, jigging her youngest on her knee, the youngest not having arrived at the age where he recognised the necessity for expressing his desires in whispers.

"Who caught them three-card-trick men after the Lewes races last year?" went on Constable Wiseman passionately. "Who has had more summonses for smoking chimneys than any other man in the force? Some people," he added as he rose heavily and took down his tunic, which hung on the wall (for Constable Wiseman invariably had tea in his shirtsleeves, even in the coldest weather, thus proving the character of his physique and his inherent homeliness) —"some people would ask to sit for promotion — but I'm perfectly satisfied. I'm not one of those ambitious sort. Why, I wouldn't know what to do with myself if they made me a sergeant."

"You deserve it, anyway," said Mrs Wiseman.

"I don't deserve anything I don't want," said Mr Wiseman loftily. "I've learnt a few things, too, but I've never made use of what's come to me officially to get me pushed along. You'll hear something in a day or two," he said mysteriously, "and in high life, too, in a manner of speaking — that is if you can call old Minute high life, which I very much doubt."

"You don't say so," said Mrs Wiseman, appropriately amazed.

Her husband nodded his head.

"There's trouble up there," he said. "From certain information I've received there has been a big row between young Mr Merril and the old man, and the CID people have been down about it. What's more," he said, "I could tell a thing or two. I've seen that boy look at the old man as though he'd like to kill him — you wouldn't believe it, would you, but I know, and it didn't happen so long ago either. He was always snubbing him when young Merril was down here acting as his secretary, and as good as called him a fool in front of my face when I served him with that summons for having his lights up – you'll hear something one of these days."

Constable Wiseman was an excellent prophet, vague as his prophecy was.

He went out of the cottage to his duty in a complacent frame of mind, which was not unusual, for Constable Wiseman was nothing if not satisfied with his fate. His complacency – circumscribed by official requirements, for the unwritten regulations of the police demand a certain attitude of mind which does not admit of a private viewpoint in business hours – continued until a little after seven o'clock that evening.

It so happened that Constable Wiseman, no less than every other member of the force on duty that night, had much to think about, much that was at once exciting and absorbing. It had been whispered before the evening parade that Sergeant Smith was to leave the force. There was some talk of his being dismissed, but it was clear that he had been given the opportunity of resigning, for he was still doing duty, which would not have been the case had he been forcibly removed.

Sergeant Smith's mien and attitude had confirmed the rumour. Nobody was surprised, since this dour officer had been in trouble before. Twice he had been before the deputy chief-constable for neglect of and being drunk whilst on duty. On the earlier occasions he had had remarkable escapes. Some people talked of influence, but it is more likely that the man's record had helped him, for he was a first-class policeman with a nose for crime, absolutely fearless, and had, moreover, assisted in the capture of one or two very desperate criminals who had made their way to the south coast town.

His last offence, however, was too grave to overlook. His inspector going the round had missed him and, after a search, he was discovered outside a public house. It is no great crime to be found outside a public house, particularly when an officer has a fairly extensive area to cover, but in this respect he was well within the limits of that area. But it must be explained that the reason the sergeant was outside the public house was because he had challenged a fellow carouser to fight, and at the moment he was discovered he was stripped to the waist and setting about his task with rare workmanlike skill.

He was also drunk.

To have retained his services thereafter would have been little less than a crying scandal. There is no doubt, however, that Sergeant Smith had made a desperate attempt to use the influence behind him, and use it to its fullest extent.

He had had one stormy interview with John Minute and had planned another. Constable Wiseman, patrolling the London road, his mind filled with the great news, was suddenly confronted with the object of his thoughts. The sergeant rode up to where the constable was standing in a professional attitude at the corner of the two roads, and jumped off.

"Wiseman," he said, and his voice was such as to suggest that he had been drinking again, "where will ye be at ten o'clock tonight?"

Constable Wiseman raised his eyes in thought.

"At ten o'clock, sergeant, I shall be opposite the gate to the cemetery."

The sergeant looked round to left and right.

"I am going to see Mr Minute on a matter of business," he said, "and you needn't mention the fact."

"I keep myself to myself," began Constable Wiseman. "What I see with one eye goes out of the other, in a manner of speaking…"

The sergeant nodded, stepped on to his bicycle again, turned it about and went at full speed down the gentle incline toward Weald Lodge. He made no secret of his visit, but rode through the wide gates up the gravel drive to the front of the house, rang the bell, and to the servant who answered, demanded peremptorily to see Mr Minute.

John Minute received him in the library, where the previous interviews had taken place. He waited until the servant had gone and the door was closed, and then he said: "Now, Crawley, there's no sense in coming to me; I can do nothing for you."

The sergeant put his helmet on the table, walked to a sideboard where a tray and a decanter stood, and poured himself out a stiff dose of whisky without invitation. John Minute watched him without any great resentment. This was not civilised Eastbourne they were in. They were back in the old free and easy days of Gwelo, where men did not expect invitations to drink.

Smith, or Crawley, to give him his real name, tossed down half a tumbler of neat whisky and turned, wiping his heavy moustache with the back of his hand.

"So you can't do anything, can't you?" he mimicked. "Well, I'm going to show you that you can and that you will!"

He put up his hand to check the words on John Minute's lips.

"There's no sense in you putting that rough stuff over me about your being able to send me to jail, because you wouldn't do it. It doesn't suit your book, John Minute, to go into court and testify against me. Too many things would come out in the witness box and you well know it – besides, Rhodesia is a long way off!"

"I know a place which isn't so far distant," said the other, looking up from his chair, "a place called Felixstowe, for example; there's another place called Cromer. I've been in consultation with a gentleman you may have heard of, a Mr Saul Arthur Mann."

"Saul Arthur Mann," repeated the other slowly. "I've never heard of him."

"You would not, but he has heard of you," said John Minute calmly. "The fact is, Crawley, there's a big bad record against you, between your serious crimes in Rhodesia and your blackmail of today. I've a few facts about you which will interest you. I know the date you came to this country, which I didn't know before, and I know how you earned your living until you found me. I know of some shares in a non-existent Rhodesian mine which you sold to a feeble-minded gentleman at Cromer and to a lady, equally feeble-minded, at Felixstowe. I've not only got the shares you sold with your signature as a director, but I have letters and receipts signed by you. It has cost me a lot of money to get them, but it was well worth it.

Crawley's face was livid. He took a step toward the other, but recoiled, for at the first hint of danger John Minute had pulled the revolver he invariably carried.

"Keep where you are, Crawley," he said. "You are close enough now to be unpleasant."

"So you've got my record, have you!" said the other with an oath. "Tucked away with your marriage lines, I'll bet, and the certificate of birth of the kids you left to starve with their mother."

"Get out of here!" said Minute, with dangerous quiet. "Get away while you're safe."

There was something in his eye which cowed the half-drunken man, who, turning with a laugh, picked up his helmet and walked from the room.

The hour was 7.35 by Constable Wiseman's watch, for slowly patrolling back, he saw the sergeant come flying out of the gateway on his bicycle and turn down toward the town. Constable Wiseman subsequently explained that he looked at his watch because he had a regular point at which he should meet Sergeant Smith at 7.45 and he was wondering whether his superior would return.

The chronology of the next three hours has been so often given in various accounts of the events which marked that evening that I may be excused if I give them in detail.

A car, with white dust, turned into the stableyard of the Star Hotel, Maidstone. The driver, in a dust-coat and a chauffeur's cap, descended and handed over the car to a garage keeper with instructions to clean it up and have it filled ready for him the following morning. He gave explicit instructions as to the number of tins of petrol he required to carry away, and tipped the garage keeper handsomely in advance.

He was described as a young man with a slight black moustache, and he was wearing his motor goggles when he went into the office of the hotel and ordered a bed and a sitting room. Therefore, his face was not seen. When his dinner was served it was remarked by the waiter that his goggles were still on his face. He gave instructions that the whole of the dinner was to be served at once and put upon the sideboard and that he did not wish to be disturbed until he rang the bell.

When the bell rang, the waiter came to find the room empty, but from the adjoining room he received orders to have breakfast by seven o'clock the following morning.

At seven o'clock the driver of the car paid his bill, his big motor goggles still upon his face, again tipped the garage keeper handsomely, and drove his car from the yard. He turned to the right and appeared to be taking the London road, but later in the day, as has been established, the car was seen on its way to Paddock Wood and was later observed at Tonbridge. The driver pulled up at a little tea house half a mile from the town, ordered sandwiches and tea, which were brought to him and which he consumed in the car.

Late in the afternoon the car was seen at Uckfield, and the theory generally held was that the driver was killing time. At the wayside cottage at which he stopped for tea – it was one of those little places that invite cyclists by an ill-printed board to tarry awhile and refresh themselves – he had some conversation with the tenant of the cottage – a widow. She seems to have been the usual loquacious friendly soul, who tells one of her business, her troubles and a fair sprinkling of the news of the day in the shortest possible time.

"I haven't seen a paper," said Rex Holland politely. "It is a very curious thing that I never thought about newspapers."

"I can get you one," said the woman eagerly; "you ought to read about that case."

"The dead chauffeur?" asked Rex Holland interestedly, for that had been the item of general news which was foremost in the woman's conversation.

"Yes, sir, he was murdered in Ashdown Forest. Many's the time I've driven over there."

"How do you know it was a murder?"

She knew for many reasons. Her brother-in-law was gamekeeper to Lord Ferring, and a colleague of his had been the man who had discovered the body, and it had appeared, as the good lady explained, that this same chauffeur was a man for whom the police had been searching in connection with a bank robbery, about which much had appeared in the newspapers of the day previous.

"How very interesting!" said Mr Holland, and took the paper from her hand.

He read the description line by line. He learnt that the police were in possession of important clues and that they were on the track of the man who had been seen in the company of the chauffeur. Moreover, said a most indiscreet newspaper writer, the police had a photograph showing the chauffeur standing by the side of his car, and reproductions of this photograph, showing the type of machine, were being circulated.

"How very interesting!" said Mr Rex Holland again, being perfectly content in his mind, for his search of the body had revealed copies of this identical picture, and the car in which he was seated was not the car which had been photographed. From this point, a mile and a half beyond Uckfield, all trace of the car and its occupant was lost.

The writer has been very careful to note the exact times and to confirm those about which there was any doubt. At 9.20 on the night when Constable Wiseman had patrolled the road before Weald Lodge and had seen Sergeant Smith flying down the road on his bicycle, and on the night of that day when Mr Rex Holland had been seen at Uckfield, there arrived by the London train, which is due at Eastbourne at 9.20, Frank Merril. The train, as a matter of fact, was three minutes late, and Frank, who had been in the latter part of the train, was one of the last of the passengers to arrive at the barrier.

When he reached the barrier, he discovered that he had no railway ticket, a very ordinary and vexatious experience, which travellers before now have endured. He searched in every pocket, including the pocket of the light ulster he wore, but without success. He was vexed, but he laughed, because he had a strong sense of humour.

"I could pay for my ticket," he smiled, "but I'll be hanged if I will! Inspector, you search that overcoat."

The amused inspector complied, whilst Frank again went through all his pockets. At his request, he accompanied the inspector to the latter's office, and there deposited on the table the contents of his pockets, his money, letters and pocket book.

"You're used to searching people," he said; "see if you can find it. I'll swear I've got it about me somewhere."

The obliging inspector felt, probed, but without success, till suddenly, with a roar of laughter, Frank cried: "What a stupid ass I am! I've got it in my hat!"

He took off his hat, and there in the lining was a first-class ticket from London to Eastbourne.

It is necessary to lay particular stress upon this incident, which had an important bearing upon subsequent events. He called a taxi cab, drove to Weald Lodge, and dismissed the driver in the road. He arrived at Weald Lodge, by the testimony of the driver and by that of Constable Wiseman, whom the car had passed, at about 9.40.

Mr John Minute at this time was alone. His suspicious nature would not allow the presence of servants in the house during his interview which he was to have with his nephew. He regarded servants as spies and eavesdroppers, and perhaps there was an excuse for his uncharitable view.

At 9.50, ten minutes after Frank had entered the gates of Weald Lodge, a car with gleaming headlights came quickly from the opposite direction and pulled up outside the gates of Weald Lodge. PC Wiseman, who at this moment was less than fifty yards from the gate, saw a man descend and pass quickly into the grounds of the house.

At 9.52 or 9.53 the constable, walking slowly toward the house, came abreast of the wall, and looking up, saw a light flash for a moment in one of the upper windows. He had hardly seen this when he heard two shots fired in rapid succession and a cry.

Only for a moment did PC Wiseman hesitate. He jumped the low wall, pushed through the shrubs and made for the side of the house from whence a flood of light fell from the open French windows of the library. He blundered into the room a pace or two, and then stopped, for the sight was one which might well arrest even as unimaginative a man as a county constable.

John Minute lay on the floor on his back, and it did not need a doctor to tell that he was dead. By his side, and almost within reach of his hand, was a revolver of a very heavy army pattern. Mechanically the constable picked up the revolver and turned his stern face to the other occupant of the room.

"This is a bad business, Mr Merril," he found his breath to say.

Frank Merril had been leaning over his uncle as the constable entered, but now stood erect, pale, but perfectly self-possessed.

"I heard the shot and I came in," he said.

"Stay where you are," said the constable, and stepping quickly out on to the lawn, he blew his whistle long and shrilly and returned to the room.

"This is a bad business, Mr Merril," he repeated.

"It is a very bad business," said the other in a low voice.

"Is that revolver yours?"

Frank shook his head.

"I've never seen it before," he said.

The Constable thought as quickly as it was humanly possible for him to think. He had no doubt in his mind that this unhappy youth had fired the shots which had ended the life of the man on the floor.

"Stay here," he said again, and again went out to blow his whistle. He walked this time on the lawn by the side of the drive towards the road. He had not taken half a dozen steps when he saw a dark figure of a man creeping stealthily along before him in the shade of the shrubs. In a second the constable was on him, had grasped him and swung him round, flashing his lantern into his prisoner's face. Instantly he released his hold.

"I beg your pardon, sergeant," he stammered.

"What's the matter?" scowled the other. "What's wrong with you, constable?"

Sergeant Smith's face was drawn and haggard. The policeman looked at him with open-mouthed astonishment.

"I didn't know it was you," he said.

"What's wrong?" asked the other again, and his voice was cracked and unnatural.

"There's been a murder – Old Minute – shot."

Sergeant Smith staggered back a pace.

"Good God!" he said. "Minute murdered! Then he did it! The young devil did it!"

"Come and have a look," invited Wiseman, recovering his balance. "I've got his nephew."

"No, no! I don't want to see John Minute dead! You go back. I'll bring another constable and a doctor."

He stumbled blindly along the drive into the road, and Constable Wiseman went back to the house. Frank was where he had left him, save that he had seated himself and was gazing steadfastly upon the dead man. He looked up as the policeman entered.

"What have you done?" he asked.

"The sergeant's gone for a doctor and another constable," said Wiseman gravely.

"I'm afraid they will be too late," said Frank. "He is…what's that?"

There was a distant hammering and a faint voice calling for help.

"What's that?" whispered Frank again.

The constable strode through the open doorway to the foot of the stairs and listened. The sound came from the upper storey. He ran upstairs, mounting two at a time, and presently located the noise. It came from an end room and somebody was hammering on the panels. The door was locked, but the key had been left in the lock and this Constable Wiseman turned, flooding the dark interior with light.

"Come out," he said, and Jasper Cole staggered out, dazed and shaking.

"Somebody hit me on the head with a sandbag," he said thickly. "I heard the shot. What has happened?"

"Mr Minute has been killed," said the policeman.

"Killed!" He fell back against the wall, his face working. "Killed!" he repeated. "Not killed!"

The constable nodded. He had found the electric switch and the passageway was illuminated.

Presently the young man mastered his emotion.

"Where is he?" he asked, and Wiseman led the way downstairs.

Jasper Cole walked into the room without a glance at Frank and bent over the dead man. For a long time he looked at him earnestly, then he turned to Frank.

"You did this!" he said. "I heard your voice and the shots! I heard you threaten him!"

Frank said nothing. He merely stared at the other and in his eyes was a look of infinite scorn.

THE CASE AGAINST FRANK MERRIL

Mr Saul Arthur Mann stood by the window of his office and moodily watched the traffic passing up and down this busy street at what was the busiest hour of the day. He stood there such a long time that the girl who had sought his help thought he must have forgotten her.

May was pale, and her pallor was emphasized by the black dress she wore. The terrible happening of a week before had left its impression upon her. For her it had been a week of sleepless nights, a week's anguish of mind unspeakable. Everybody had been most kind and Jasper was as gentle as a woman. Such was the influence that he exercised over her that she did not feel any sense of resentment against him, even though she knew that he was the principal witness for the Crown. He was so sincere, so honest in his sympathy, she told herself.

He was so free from any bitterness against the man whom he believed had killed his best friend and his most generous employer that she could not sustain the first feeling of resentment she had felt. Perhaps it was because her great sorrow overshadowed all other emotions, yet she was free to analyse her friendship with the man who was working day and night to send the man who loved her to a felon's doom. She could not understand herself; still less could she understand Jasper.

She looked up again at Mr Mann as he stood by the window, his hands clasped behind him, and as she did so, he turned slowly and came back to where she sat. His usually jocund face was lugubrious and worried.

"I have given more thought to this matter than I've given to any other problem I have tackled," he said. "I believe Mr Merril to be falsely accused, and I have one or two points to make to his counsel which, when they are brought forward in Court, will prove beyond any doubt whatever that he was innocent. I don't believe that matters are so black against him as you think. The other side will certainly bring forward the forgery and the doctored books to supply a motive for the murder. Inspector Nash is in charge of the case and he promised to call here at four o'clock."

He looked at his watch.

"It wants three minutes. Have you any suggestion to offer?"

She shook her head.

"I can floor the prosecution," Mr Mann went on, "but what I cannot do is to find the murderer for certain. It is obviously one of three men. It is either Sergeant Crawley, alias Smith, about whose antecedents Mr Minute made an inquiry, or Jasper Cole, the secretary, or – "

He shrugged his shoulders.

It was not necessary to say who was the third suspect.

There came a knock at the door and the commissionaire announced Inspector Nash. That stout and stoical officer gave a non-committal nod to Mr Mann and a smiling recognition to the girl.

"Well, you know how matters stand, Inspector," said Mr Mann briskly, "and I thought I'd ask you to come here today to straighten a few things out."

"It is rather irregular, Mr Mann," said the Inspector; "but as they've no objection at headquarters, I don't mind telling you, within limits, all that I know, but I don't suppose I can tell you any more than you have found out for yourself."

"Do you really think Mr Merril committed this crime?" asked the girl.

The Inspector raised his eyebrows and pursed his lips.

"It looks uncommonly like it, miss," he said. "We have evidence that the bank has been robbed, and it is almost certainly proved that Merril had access to the books and was the only person in the bank who could have faked the figures and transferred the money from one account to another without being found out. There are still one or two doubtful points to be cleared up, but there is the motive, and when you've got the motive you are three parts on your way to finding the criminal. It isn't a straightforward case by any means," he confessed, "and the more I go into it, the more puzzled I am. I don't mind telling you this frankly. I have seen Constable Wiseman, who swears that at the moment the shots were fired he saw a light flash in the upper window. We have the statement of Mr Cole that he was in his room, his employer having requested that he should make himself scarce when the nephew came, and he tells us how somebody opened the door quietly and flashed an electric torch upon him."

"What was Cole doing in the dark?" asked Mann quickly.

"He had a headache and was lying down," said the Inspector. "When he saw the light he jumped up and made for it, and was immediately 'slugged'; the door closed upon him and was locked. Between his leaving the bed and reaching the door he heard Mr Merril's voice threatening his uncle and the shots. Immediately afterwards he was rendered insensible."

"A curious story!" said Saul Arthur Mann dryly. "A very curious story!"

The girl felt an unaccountable and altogether amazing desire to defend Jasper against the innuendo in the other's tone, and it was with difficulty that she restrained herself.

"I don't think it is a good story," said the Inspector frankly, "but that is between ourselves. And then, of course," he went on, "we have the remarkable behaviour of Sergeant Smith."

"Where is he?" asked Mr Mann.

The Inspector shrugged his shoulders.

"Sergeant Smith has disappeared," he said, "though I dare say we shall find him before long. He is the only one – the most puzzling element of all is the fourth man concerned, the man who arrived in the motorcar and who was evidently Mr Rex Holland. We have got a very full description of him."

"I also have a very full description of him," said Mr Mann quietly, "but I've been unable to identify him with any of the people in my records."

"Anyway, it was his car, there is no doubt about that."

"And he was the murderer," said Mr Mann. "I've no doubt about that, nor have you."

"I have doubts about everything," replied the Inspector diplomatically.

"What was in the car?" asked the little man brightly. He was rapidly recovering his good humour.

"That I'm afraid I cannot tell you," smiled the detective.

"Then I'll tell you," said Saul Arthur Mann, and stepping up to his desk, took a memorandum from a drawer. "There were two motor-rugs, two holland coats – one white, one brown. There were two sets of motor goggles. There was a package of revolver cartridges, from which six had been extracted, a leather revolver holster, a small garden trowel, and one or two other little things."

Inspector Nash swore softly under his breath.

"I'm blessed if I know how you found all that out," he said, with a little asperity in his voice. "The car was not touched or searched until we came on the scene, and beyond myself and Sergeant Mannering of my department, nobody knows what the car contained."

Saul Arthur Mann smiled, and it was a very happy and triumphant smile.

"You see, I know!" he purred. "That is one point in Merril's favour."

"Yes," agreed the detective, and smiled.

"Why do you smile, Mr Nash?" asked the little man suspiciously.

"I was thinking of a county policeman who seems to have some extraordinary theories on the subject."

"Oh, you mean Wiseman," said Mann with a grin. "I've interviewed that gentleman. There is a great detective lost in him, Inspector."

"It is lost all right," said the detective laconically. "Wiseman is very certain that Merril committed the crime, and I think you are going to have a difficulty in persuading a jury that he didn't. You see, Merril's story is that he came and saw his uncle, that they had a few minutes' chat together, that his uncle suddenly had an attack of faintness and that he went out of the room into the dining room to get a glass of water. Whilst he was in the dining room, he heard the shots and came running back, still with the glass in his hand, and saw his uncle lying on the ground. I saw the glass, which was half-filled. I was also there in time to examine the dining room and see that Mr Merril had spilt some of the water when he was taking it from the carafe. All that part of the story is circumstantially sound. What we cannot understand, and what a jury will never understand, is how in the very short space of time the murderer could have got into the room and made his escape again."

"The French windows were open," said Mr Mann; "all the evidence that we have is to this effect, including the evidence of PC Wiseman."

"In these circumstances how comes it that the constable, who, when he heard the shot, made straight for the room, did not meet the murderer escaping? He saw nobody in the grounds – "

"Except Sergeant Smith, or Crawley," interspersed Saul Arthur Mann readily. "I have reason to believe, and indeed, reason to know, that Sergeant Smith, or Crawley, had a motive for being in the house. I supplied Mr Minute, who was a client of mine, with certain documents, and those documents were in the safe in his bedroom. What is more likely than that this Crawley, to whom it was vitally necessary that the documents in question should be recovered, should have entered the house in search of those documents? I don't mind telling you that they related to a fraud of which he was the author, and they were in themselves all the proof which the police would require to obtain a conviction against him. He was obviously the man who struck down Mr Cole and whose light the constable saw flashing in the upper window."

"In that case he cannot have been the murderer," said the detective quickly, "because the shots were fired while he was still in the room.

They were almost simultaneous with the appearance of the flash at the upper window."

"H'm!" said Saul Arthur Mann, for the moment nonplussed.

"The more you go into this matter, the more complicated does it become," said the police officer with a shake of his head, "and to my mind, the clearer is the case against Merril."

"With this reservation," interrupted the other, "that you have to account for the movements of Mr Rex Holland, who comes on the scene ten minutes after Frank Merril arrives and who leaves his car. He leaves his car for a very excellent reason," he went on. "Sergeant Smith, who runs away to get assistance, meets two men of the Sussex Constabulary, hurrying in response to Wiseman's whistle. One of them stands by the car and the other comes into the house. It was therefore impossible for the murderer to make use of the car. Here is another point I would have you explain."

He had hoisted himself on the edge of his desk and sat, an amusing little figure, his legs swinging a foot from the ground.

"The revolver used was a big Webley, not an easy thing to carry or conceal about your person, and undoubtedly brought to the scene of the crime by the man in the car. You will say that Merril, who wore an overcoat, might have easily brought it in his pocket; but the absolute proof that that could not have been the case is that, on his arrival by train from London, Mr Merril lost his ticket and very carefully searched himself, a railway inspector assisting, to discover the bit of pasteboard. He turned out everything he had in his pocket in the inspector's presence, and his overcoat – the only place where he could have concealed such a heavy weapon – was searched by the inspector himself."

The detective nodded.

"It is a very difficult case," he agreed, "and one in which I've no great heart; for, to be absolutely honest, my views are that, whilst it might have been Merril, the balance of proof is that it was not. That is, of course, my unofficial view, and I shall work pretty hard to secure a conviction."

"I am sure you will," said Mr Mann heartily.

"Must the case go into the Court?" asked the girl anxiously.

"There is no other way for it," replied the officer. "You see, we have arrested him, and unless something turns up the magistrate must commit him for trial on the evidence we have secured."

"Poor Frank," she said softly.

"It is rough on him if he's innocent," agreed Nash, "but it is lucky for him if he's guilty. My experience of crime and criminals is that it is generally the obvious man who commits the crime; only once in fifty years is he innocent, whether he is acquitted or whether he is found guilty."

He offered his hand to Mr Mann.

"I'll be getting along now, sir," he said. "The Commissioner asked me to give you all the assistance I possibly could, and I hope I have done so."

"What are you doing in the case of Jasper Cole?" asked Mann quickly.

The detective smiled.

"You ought to know, sir," he said, and was amused at his own little joke.

"Well, young lady," said Mann, turning to the girl after the detective had gone. "I think you know how matters stand. Nash suspects Cole."

"Jasper!" she said in shocked surprise.

"Jasper," he repeated.

"But that is impossible. He was locked in his room."

"That doesn't make it impossible. I know of fourteen distinct cases of men who committed crimes and were able to lock themselves in their rooms, leaving the key outside. There was a case of Henry Burton, coiner, there was William Francis Rector who killed a warder whilst in prison and locked the cell upon himself from the inside. There was – but there, why should I bother you with instances? That kind of trick is common enough. No," he said, "it is the motive that we have to find. Do you still want me to go with you tomorrow, Miss Nuttall?" he asked.

"I should be very glad if you would," she said earnestly. "Poor dear uncle! I didn't think I could ever enter the house again."

"I can relieve your mind about that," he said; "the will is not to be read in the house. Mr Minute's lawyers have arranged for the reading at their offices in Lincoln's Inn Fields. I have the address here somewhere."

He fumbled in his pocket and took out a card.

"Power, Commons and Co.," he read, "194, Lincoln's Inn Fields. I will meet you there at three o'clock."

He rumpled his untidy hair with an embarrassed laugh. I seem to have drifted into the position of guardian to you, young lady," he said. "I can't say that it is an unpleasant task, although it is a great responsibility."

"You have been splendid, Mr Mann," she said warmly, "and I shall never forget all you have done for me. Somehow I feel that Frank will get off, and I hope – I pray, that it will not be at Jasper's expense."

He looked at her in surprise and disappointment.

"I thought – " He stopped.

"You thought I was engaged to Frank, and so I am," she said with heightened colour; "but Jasper is – I hardly know how to put it."

"I see," said Mr Mann, though if the truth be told, he saw nothing which enlightened him.

Punctually at three o'clock the next afternoon they walked up the steps of the lawyer's office together. Jasper Cole was already there, and to Mr Mann's surprise so also was Inspector Nash, who explained his presence in a few words.

"There may be something in the will which will open a new viewpoint," he said.

Mr Power, the solicitor, an elderly man inclined to rotundity, was introduced, and taking his position before the fireplace opened the proceedings with an expression of regret as to the circumstances which had brought them together.

"The will of my late client," he said, "was not drawn up by me. It was written in Mr Minute's handwriting and revokes the only other will, one which was prepared some four years ago, and which made provisions rather different from those in the present instrument. This will" – he took a single sheet of paper out of an envelope – "was made last year and was witnessed by Thomas Wellington Crawley" – he adjusted his pince-nez and examined the signature – "late trooper of the Matabeleland Mounted Police, and by George Warrell, who was Mr Minute's butler at the time. Warrell died in the Eastbourne Hospital in the spring of this year."

There was a deep silence. Saul Arthur Mann's face was eagerly thrust forward, his head turned slightly to one side. Inspector Nash showed an unusual amount of interest. Both men had the same thought, a new will witnessed by two people, one of whom was dead and the other a fugitive from justice – what did this will contain?

It was the briefest of documents. To his ward he left the sum of £200,000, "a provision which was also made in the previous will, I might add," said the lawyer, and to this he added all his shares in the Gwelo Deep.

To his nephew, Francis Merril, he left £20,000.

The lawyer paused and looked round the little circle, and then continued: "The residue of my property, movable and immovable, all my furniture, leases, shares, cash at bankers, and all interests whatsoever, I bequeath to Jasper Cole, so called, who is at present my secretary and confidential agent."

The detective and Saul Arthur Mann exchanged glances and Nash's lips moved.

"How is that for a 'motive'?" he whispered.

THE TRIAL OF FRANK MERRIL

The trial of Frank Merril, on the charge that he "did on the twenty-eighth day of June, in the year of our Lord one thousand nine hundred, wilfully and wickedly kill and slay by a pistol shot John Minute," was the sensation of a season which was unusually prolific in murder trials. The trial took place at the Lewes Assizes in a crowded courtroom and lasted, as we know, for sixteen days, five days of which were given to the examination in chief and the cross-examination of the accountants who had gone into the books of the bank.

The prosecution endeavoured to establish the fact that no other person but Frank Merril could have access to the books, and that, therefore, no other person could have falsified them or manipulated the transfer of monies. It cannot be said that the prosecution had wholly succeeded, for when Brandon, the bank manager, was put into the box, he was compelled to admit that not only Frank, but he himself and Jasper Cole were in a position to reach the books.

The opening speech for the Crown had been a masterly one. But that there were many weak points in the evidence and in the assumptions which the prosecution drew, was evident to the merest tyro.

Sir George Murphy Jackson, the Attorney-General, who prosecuted, attempted to dispose summarily of certain conflictions, and it had to be confessed that his explanations were very plausible.

"The defence will tell us," he said in that shrill, clarion tone of his which has made to quake the hearts of so many hostile witnesses, "that we have not accounted for the fourth man who drove up in his car ten minutes after Merril had entered the house and disappeared, but I am going to tell you my theory of that incident."

"Merril had an accomplice who is not in custody, and that accomplice is Rex Holland. Merril had planned and prepared this murder, because from some statement which his uncle had made, he believed that not only was his whole future dependent upon destroying his benefactor and silencing for ever the one man who knew the extent of his villainy, but he had in his cold, shrewd way accurately foreseen the exact consequence of such a shooting. It was a big criminal's big idea. He foresaw this trial," he said impressively: "he foresaw, gentlemen of the jury, his acquittal at your hands. He foresaw a reaction which would not only give him the woman he professes to love, but, in consequence, place in his hands the disposal of her considerable fortune. Why should he shoot John Minute? you may ask, and I reply to that question with another. What would have happened had he not shot his uncle? He would have been a ruined man. The doors of his uncle's house would have been closed to him. The legacy would have been revoked, the marriage for which he had planned so long would have been an unrealized dream. He knew the extent of the fortune which was coming to Miss Nuttall. Mr Minute made two wills, in both of which he left an identical sum to his ward. The first of these, revoked by the second and containing the same provision, was witnessed by the man in the dock. He knew, too, that the Rhodesian gold mine, the shares of which were held by John Minute on the girl's behalf, was likely to prove a very rich proposition, and I suggest that the information coming to him as Mr Minute's secretary, he deliberately suppressed that information for his own purpose.

"What had he to gain? I ask you to believe that, if he is acquitted on this charge, he will have achieved all that he ever hoped to achieve."

There was a little murmur in the court. Frank Merril, leaning on the edge of the dock, looked down at the girl in the body of the court, and their eyes met. He saw the indignation in her face and nodded with a little smile, then turned again to the counsel with that eager, half-quizzical look of interest which the girl had so often seen upon his handsome face.

"Much will be made, in the course of this trial, of the presence of another man, and the defence will endeavour to secure capital out of the fact that the man Crawley, who, it was suggested, was in the house for an improper purpose, has not yet been discovered. As to the fourth man, the driver of the motorcar, there seems little doubt that he was an accomplice of Merril. This mysterious Rex Holland, who has been identified by Mrs Totney of Uckfield, spent the whole of the day wandering about Sussex, obviously having one plan in his mind, which was to arrive at Mr Minute's house at the same time as his confederate.

"You will have the taxi driver's evidence that when Merril stepped down after being driven from the station, he looked left and right, as though he were expecting somebody. The plan to some extent miscarried. The accomplice arrived ten minutes too late. On some pretext or other Merril probably left the room. I suggest that he did not go into the dining room, but that he went out into the garden and was met by his accomplice, who handed him the weapon with which this crime was committed.

"It may be asked by the defence why the accomplice, who was presumably Rex Holland, did not himself commit the crime. I could offer two or three alternative suggestions, all of which are feasible. The deceased man was shot at close quarters, and was found in such an attitude as to suggest that he was wholly unprepared for the attack. We know that he was in some fear and that he invariably went armed, yet it is fairly certain that he made no attempt to draw his weapon, which he certainly would have done had he been suddenly confronted by an armed stranger.

"I do not pretend that I am explaining the strange relationship between Merril and this mysterious forger. Merril is the only man who has seen him and has given a vague and somewhat confused description of him. 'He was a man with a short, close-clipped beard' is Merril's description. The woman who served him with tea near Uckfield describes him as a 'youngish man with a dark moustache, but otherwise clean-shaven.' There is no reason, of course, why he should not have removed his beard, but as against that suggestion, we will call evidence to prove that the man seen driving with the murdered chauffeur was invariably a man with a moustache and no beard, so that the balance of probability is on the side of the supposition that Merril is not telling the truth. An unknown client with a large deposit at his bank would not be likely to constantly alter his appearance. If he were a criminal, as we know him to be, there would be another reason why he should not excite suspicion in this way."

His address covered the greater part of a day – but he returned to the scene in the garden; to the supposed meeting of the two men and to the murder.

Saul Arthur Mann, sitting with Frank's solicitor, scratched his nose and grinned.

"I have never heard of a more ingenious piece of reconstruction," he said, "though, of course, the whole thing is palpably absurd."

As a theory it was, no doubt, excellent, but men are not sentenced to death on theories, however ingenious they may be. Probably nobody in the court so completely admired the ingenuity as the man most affected. At the lunch interval on the day on which this theory was put forward he met his solicitor and Saul Arthur Mann in the bare room in which such interviews are permitted.

"It was really fascinating to hear him," said Frank, as he sipped the cup of tea which they had brought him. "I almost began to believe that I had committed the murder! But isn't it rather alarming? Will the jury take the same view?" he asked, a little troubled.

The solicitor shook his head.

"Unsupported theories of that sort do not go well with juries, and of course the whole story is so flimsy and so improbable that it will go for no more than a piece of clever reasoning."

"Did anybody see you at the railway station?"

Frank shook his head.

"I suppose hundreds of people saw me, but would hardly remember me."

"Was there anyone on the train who knew you?"

"No," said Frank after a moment's thought. "There were six people in my carriage until we got to Lewes; but I think I told you that and you have not succeeded in tracing any of them."

"It is most difficult to get into touch with those people," said the lawyer. "Think of the scores of people one travels with, without ever remembering what they looked like or how they were dressed. If you had been a woman, travelling with women, every one of your fellow-passengers would have remembered you and would have recalled your hat!"

Frank laughed.

"There are certain disadvantages in being a man," he said. "How do you think the case is going?"

"They have offered no evidence yet. I think you will agree, Mr Mann," he said respectfully, for Saul Arthur Mann was a power in legal circles.

"None at all," the little fellow agreed.

Frank recalled the first day he had seen him with his hat perched on the back of his head and his shabby, genteel exterior.

"Oh, by Jove," he said, "I suppose they will be trying to fasten that death of that man upon me, that we saw in Gray Square!"

Saul Arthur Mann nodded.

"They have not put that in the indictment," he said, "nor the case of the chauffeur. You see, your conviction will rest entirely upon this present charge, and both the other matters are subsidiary."

Frank walked thoughtfully up and down the room, his hands behind his back.

"I wonder who Rex Holland is?" he said, half to himself.

"You still have your theory?" asked the lawyer, eyeing him keenly.

Frank nodded.

"And you still would rather not put it into words?"

"Much rather not," said Frank gravely.

He returned to the court and glanced round for the girl, but she was not there. The rest of the afternoon's proceedings, taken up as they were with the preliminaries of the case, bored him.

It was on the twelfth day of the trial that Jasper Cole stepped on to the witness stand. He was dressed in black and was paler than usual, but he took the oath in a firm voice and answered the questions which were put to him without hesitation.

The story of Frank's quarrel with his uncle, of the forged cheques and of his own experience on the night of the crime, filled the greater part of the forenoon, and it was in the afternoon when Bryan Bennett, one of the most brilliant barristers of his time, stood up to cross-examine.

"Had you any suspicion that your employer was being robbed?"

"I had a suspicion," replied Jasper.

"Did you communicate your suspicion to your employer?"

Jasper hesitated.

"No," he replied at last.

"Why do you hesitate?" asked Bennett sharply.

"Because, although I did not directly communicate my suspicions, I hinted to Mr Minute that he should have an independent audit."

"So you thought the books were wrong?"

"I did."

"In these circumstances," asked Bennett slowly, "do you not think it was very unwise of you to touch those books yourself?"

"When did I touch them?" asked Jasper quickly.

"I suggest that on a certain night you came to the bank and remained in the bank by yourself, examining the ledgers on behalf of your employer, and that during that time you handled at least three books in which these falsifications were made."

"That is quite correct," said Jasper, after a moment's thought, "but my suspicions were general and did not apply to any particular group of books."

"But did you not think it was dangerous?"

Again the hesitation.

"It may have been foolish, and if I had known how matters were developing I should certainly not have touched them."

"You do admit that there were several periods of time from 7 in the evening until 9 and from 9.30 until 11.15 when you were absolutely alone in the bank."

"That is true," said Jasper.

"And during those periods you could, had you wished and had you been a forger, for example, or had you any reason for falsifying the entries, have made those falsifications?"

"I admit there was time," said Jasper.

"Would you describe yourself as a friend of Frank Merril's?"

"Not a close friend," replied Jasper.

"Did you like him?"

"I cannot say that I was fond of him," was the reply.

"He was a rival of yours?"

"In what respect?"

Counsel shrugged his shoulders.

"He was very fond of Miss Nuttall."

"Yes."

"And she was fond of him."

"Yes."

"Did you not aspire to pay your addresses to Miss Nuttall?"

Jasper Cole looked down to the girl and May averted her eyes. Her cheeks were burning and she had a wild desire to flee from the court.

"If you mean, did I love Miss Nuttall," said Jasper Cole in his quiet, even tone, "I reply that I did."

"You even secured the active support of Mr Minute?"

"I never urged the matter with Mr Minute," said Jasper.

"So that if he moved on your behalf he did so without your knowledge?"

"Without my preknowledge," corrected the witness; "he told me afterwards that he had spoken to Miss Nuttall and I was considerably embarrassed."

"I understand you were a man of curious habits, Mr Cole."

"We are all people of curious habits," smiled the witness.

"But you in particular. You were an Orientalist, I believe?"

"I have studied Oriental languages and customs," said Jasper shortly.

"Have you ever extended your study to the realm of hypnotism?"

"I have," replied the witness.

"Have you ever made experiments?"

"On animals, yes."

"On human beings?"

"No, I have never made experiments on human beings."

"Have you also made a study of narcotics?"

The lawyer leant forward over the table and looked at the witness between half-closed eyes.

"I have made experiments with narcotic herbs and plants," said Jasper, after a moment's hesitation. "I think that you should know that the career which was planned for me was that of a doctor, and I have always been very interested in the effects of narcotics."

"You know of a drug called *cannabis indica*?" asked the counsel consulting his paper.

"Yes, it is 'Indian hemp.' "

"Is there an infusion of *cannabis indica* to be obtained?"

"I do not think there is," said the other. "I can probably enlighten you, because I see now the trend of your examination. I once told Frank Merril, many years ago when I was very enthusiastic, that an infusion of *cannabis indica* combined with tincture of opium and hyocine produced certain effects."

"It is inclined to sap the will power of a man or a woman who is constantly absorbing this poison in small doses," suggested the counsel.

"That is so."

The counsel now switched off on a new tack.

"Do you know the East of London?"

"Yes, slightly."

"Do you know Silver Rents?"

"Yes."

"Do you ever go to Silver Rents?"

"Yes, I go there very regularly."

The readiness of the reply astonished both Frank and the girl. She had been feeling more and more uncomfortable as the cross-examination continued, and had a feeling that she had in some way betrayed Jasper Cole's confidence. She had listened to the cross-examination which revealed Jasper as a scientist with something approaching amazement. She had known of the laboratory, but had associated the place with those entertaining experiments that an idle dabbler in chemistry might undertake.

For a moment she doubted and searched her mind for some occasion when he had practised his medical knowledge. Dimly she realised that there *had* been some such occasion, and then she remembered that it had always been Jasper Cole who had concocted the strange draughts which had so relieved the headache to which, when she was a little younger, she had been something of a martyr. Could he – she struggled hard to dismiss the thought as being unworthy of her, and now, when the object of his visits to Silver Rents was under examination, she found her curiosity growing.

"Why did you go to Silver Rents?"

There was no answer.

"I will repeat my question. With what object did you go to Silver Rents?"

"I decline to answer that question," said the man in the box coolly. "I merely tell you that I went there frequently."

"And you refuse to say why?"

"I refuse to say why," repeated the witness.

The judge on the bench made a little note.

"I put it to you," said counsel, speaking impressively, "that it was in Silver Rents that you took on another identity."

"That is probably true," said the other, and the girl gasped. He was so cool, so self-possessed, so sure of himself.

"I suggest to you," the counsel went on, "that in those Rents Jasper Cole became Rex Holland."

There was a buzz of excitement, a sudden soft clamour of voices through which the usher's harsh demand for silence cut like a knife.

"Your suggestion is an absurd one," said Jasper without heat, "and I presume that you are going to produce evidence to support so infamous a statement."

"What evidence I produce," said counsel with asperity, "is a matter for me to decide."

"It is also a matter for the witness," interposed the soft voice of the judge. "As you have suggested that Holland was a party to the murder, and as you are inferring that Rex Holland is Jasper Cole, it is presumed that you will call evidence to support so serious a charge."

"I am not prepared to call evidence, my lord, and if your lordship thinks the question should not have been put I am willing to withdraw it."

The judge nodded and turned his head to the jury.

"You will consider that question as not having been put, gentlemen," he said. "Doubtless counsel is trying to establish the fact that one person might just as easily have been Rex Holland as another. There is no suggestion that Mr Cole went to Silver Rents – which I understand is in a very poor neighbourhood – with any illegal intent, or that he was committing any crime or behaving in any way improperly by paying such frequent visits. There may be something in the witness' life associated with that poor house which has no bearing on the case and which he does not desire should be ventilated in this court. It happens to many of us," the judge went on, "that we have associations which it would embarrass us to reveal."

This little incident closed that portion of the cross-examination and counsel went on to the night of the murder. "When did you come to the house?" he asked.

"I came to the house soon after dark."

"Had you been in London?"

"Yes, I walked from Bexhill."

"It was dark when you arrived?"

"Yes, nearly dark."

"The servants had all gone out?"

"Yes."

"Was Mr Minute pleased to see you?"

"Yes, he had expected me earlier in the day."

"Did he tell you that his nephew was coming to see him?"

"I knew that."

"You say he suggested that you should make yourself scarce?"

"Yes."

"And as you had a headache, you went upstairs and lay down on your bed?"

"Yes."

"What were you doing in Bexhill?"

"I came down from town and got into the wrong portion of the train."

A junior leaned over and whispered quickly to his leader.

"I see, I see," said the counsel petulantly. "Your ticket was found at Bexhill. Have you ever seen Mr Rex Holland?" he asked.

"Never."

"You have never met any person of that name?"

"Never."

In this tame way the cross-examination closed as cross examinations have a habit of doing.

By the time the final addresses of counsel had ended and the judge had finished a masterly summing-up, there was no doubt whatever in the mind of any person in the court as to what the verdict would be. The jury was absent from the box for twenty minutes and returned a verdict of: "Not Guilty!"

The judge discharged Frank Merril without comment, and he left the court a free but ruined man.

THE MAN WHO CAME TO MONTREUX

It was two months after the great trial, on a warm day in October when Frank Merril stepped ashore from the big white paddle-boat which had carried him across Lake Leman from Lausanne, and handing his bag to a porter, made his way to the hotel omnibus. He looked at his watch. It pointed to a quarter to four, and May was not due to arrive until half-past. He went to his hotel, washed and changed, and came down to the vestibule to inquire if the instructions he had telegraphed had been carried out.

May was arriving in company with Saul Arthur Mann, who was taking one of his rare holidays abroad. Frank had seen the girl only once since the day of the trial. He had come to breakfast on the following morning and very little had been said. He was due to leave that afternoon for the Continent. He had a little money, sufficient for his needs, and Jasper Cole had offered no suggestion that he would dispute the will in so far as it affected Frank. So he had gone abroad and had idled away two months in France, Spain and Italy, and had then made his leisurely way back to Switzerland by way of Maggiore.

He had grown a little graver, was a little more set in his movements, but he bore upon his face no mark to indicate the mental agony through which he must have passed in that long-drawn-out and wearisome trial. So thought the girl, as she came through the swing doors of the hotel, passed the obsequious hotel servants and greeted him in the big palm-court.

If she saw any change in him, he remarked a development in her which was a little short of wonderful. She was at that age when the

117

woman is breaking through the beautiful chrysalis of girlhood. In those two months a remarkable change had come over her, a change which he could not for the moment define, for this phenomenon of development had been denied to his experience.

"Why, May," he said, "you are quite old."

She laughed and again he noticed the change. The laugh was richer, sweeter, purer than the bubbling treble he had known.

"You are not getting complimentary, are you?" she asked.

She was exquisitely dressed and had that poise which few English women achieve. She had the art of wearing clothes, and from the flimsy crest of her toque to the tips of her little feet she was all that the most exacting critic could desire. There are well-dressed women who are no more than mannequins. There are fine ladies, who cannot be mistaken for anything but fine ladies, whose dresses are a horror and an abomination and whose expressed tastes are execrable.

May Nuttall was a fine lady, finely apparelled.

"When you have finished admiring me, Frank," she said, "tell us what you have been doing. But first of all let us have some tea. You know Mr Mann?"

The little investigator beaming in the background took Frank's hand and shook it heartily. He was dressed in what he thought was an appropriate costume for a mountainous country. His boots were stout, the woollen stockings which covered his very thin legs were very woollen, and his knickerbocker suit was warranted to stand wear and tear. He had abandoned his top hat for a large golf cap which was perched rakishly over one eye. Frank looked round apprehensively for Saul Arthur's alpenstock, and was relieved when he failed to discover one.

The girl threw off her fur wrap and unbuttoned her gloves as the waiter placed the big silver tray on the table before her.

"I'm afraid I have not much to tell," said Frank in answer to her question. "I've just been loafing around. What is your news?"

"What is my news?" she asked. "I don't think I have any, except that everything is going very smoothly in England, and oh, Frank, I am so immensely rich."

He smiled.

"The appropriate thing would be to say that I am immensely poor," he said, "but as a matter of fact I am not. I went down to Aix and won quite a lot of money."

'Won it?" she said.

He nodded with an amused little smile.

"You wouldn't have thought that I was a gambler, would you?" he asked solemnly. "I don't think I am, as a matter of fact, but somehow I wanted to occupy my mind."

"I understand," she said quickly.

Another little pause while she poured out the tea, which afforded Saul Arthur Mann an opportunity of firing off fifty facts about Geneva in as many sentences.

"What has happened to Jasper?" asked Frank after a while.

The girl flushed a little.

"Oh, Jasper," she said awkwardly. "I see him, you know. He has become more mysterious than ever, quite like one of those wicked people one reads about in sensational stories. He has a laboratory somewhere in the country and he does quite a lot of motoring. I've seen him several times at Brighton, for instance."

Frank nodded slowly.

"I should think that he was a good driver," he said.

Saul Arthur Mann looked up and met his eye with a smile which was lost upon the girl.

"He has been kind to me," she said hesitatingly.

"Does he ever speak about − ?"

She shook her head.

"I don't want to think about that," she said. "Please don't let us talk about it."

He knew she was referring to John Minute's death and changed the conversation.

A few minutes later he had an opportunity of speaking with Mr Mann.

'What is the news?" he asked.

Saul Arthur Mann looked round.

"I think we are getting near the truth," he said, dropping his voice. "One of my men has had him under observation ever since the day of the trial. There is no doubt that he is really a brilliant chemist."

"Have you a theory?"

"I have several," said Mr Mann. "I am perfectly satisfied that the unfortunate fellow we saw together on the occasion of our first meeting was Rex Holland's servant. I was as certain that he was poisoned by a very powerful poison. When your trial was on the body was exhumed and examined, and the presence of that drug was discovered. It was the same as that employed in the case of the chauffeur. Obviously, Rex Holland is a clever chemist. I wanted to see you about that. He said at the trial that he had discussed such matters with you."

Frank nodded.

"We used to have quite long talks about drugs," he said. "I have recalled many of those conversations since the day of the trial. He even fired me with his enthusiasm and I used to assist him in his little experiments, and obtained quite a working knowledge of these particular elements. Unfortunately I cannot remember very much, for my enthusiasm soon died, and beyond the fact that he employed hyocine and Indian hemp I have only the dimmest recollection of any of the constituents he employed."

Saul Arthur nodded energetically.

"I shall have more to tell you later, perhaps," he said, "but at present my inquiries are shaping quite nicely. He is going to be a difficult man to catch, because, if all I believe is true, he is one of the most cold-blooded and calculating men it has ever been my lot to meet – and I have met a few," he added grimly.

When he said men, Frank knew that he had meant criminals.

"We are probably doing him a horrible injustice," he smiled; "poor old Jasper!"

"You are not cut out for police work," snapped Saul Arthur Mann, "you've too many sympathies."

"I don't exactly sympathise," rejoined Frank, "but I just pity him in a way."

Again Mr Mann looked round cautiously and again lowered his voice, which had risen.

"There is one thing I want to talk to you about. It is rather a delicate matter, Mr Merril," he said.

"Fire ahead."

"It is about Miss Nuttall. She has seen a lot of our friend Jasper, and after every interview she seems to grow more and more reliant upon his help. Once or twice she has been embarrassed when I have spoken about Jasper Cole, and has changed the subject."

Frank pursed his lips thoughtfully, and a hard little look came into his eyes which did not promise well for Jasper.

"So that is it," he said, and shrugged his shoulders. "If she cares for him it is not my business."

"But it *is* your business," said the other sharply. "She was fond enough of you to offer to marry you."

Further talk was cut short by the arrival of the girl. Their meeting at Geneva had been to some extent a chance one. She was going through to Chamonix to spend the winter, and Saul Arthur Mann seized the opportunity of taking a short and a pleasant holiday. Hearing that Frank was in Switzerland, she had telegraphed him to meet her.

"Are you staying any time in Switzerland?" she asked him as they strolled along the beautiful quay.

"I am going back to London tonight," he replied.

"Tonight?" she said in surprise.

He nodded.

"But I am staying for two or three days," she protested.

"I intended also staying two or three days," he smiled, "but my business will not wait."

Nevertheless, she persuaded him to stay till the morrow.

They were at breakfast when the morning mail was delivered, and Frank noted that she went rapidly through the dozen letters which came to her and she chose one for first reading. He could not help but see that it bore an English stamp and his long acquaintance with the curious calligraphy of Jasper Cole left him in no doubt as to who was the correspondent. He saw with what eagerness she read the letter, the little look of disappointment when she turned to an inside sheet and found that it had not been filled, and his mind was made up. He had a post also, which he examined with some evidence of impatience.

"Your mail is not as nice as mine," said the girl with a smile.

"It is not nice at all," he grumbled. "The one thing I wanted, and to be very truthful, May, the one inducement – "

"To stay over the night," she added, "was – what?"

"I have been trying to buy a house on the lake," he said, "and the infernal agent at Lausanne promised to write telling me whether my terms had been agreed to by his client."

He looked down at the table and frowned. Saul Arthur Mann had a great and extensive knowledge of human nature. He had remarked the disappointment on Frank's face, having identified also the correspondent whose letter claimed priority of attention. He knew that Frank's anger with the house agent was very likely the expression of his anger in quite another direction.

"Can I send the letter on?" suggested the girl.

"That won't help me," said Frank, with a little grimace. "I wanted to settle the business this week."

"I have it," she said. "I will open the letter and telegraph to you in Paris whether the terms are accepted or not."

Frank laughed.

"It hardly seems worth that," he said, "but I should take it as awfully kind of you if you would, May."

Saul Arthur Mann believed in his mind that Frank did not care twopence whether the agent accepted the terms or not, but that he had taken this as a heaven-sent opportunity for veiling his annoyance.

"You have had quite a large mail, Miss Nuttall," he said.

"I've only opened one, though. It is from Jasper," she said hurriedly.

Again both men noticed the faint flush, the strange, unusual light which came to her eyes.

"And where does Jasper write from?" asked Frank, steadying his voice.

"He writes from England, but he was going on to the Continent to Holland the day he wrote," she said. "It is funny to think that he is here."

"In Switzerland?" asked Frank in surprise.

"Don't be silly," she laughed. "No, I mean on the mainland – I mean there is no sea between us."

She went crimson.

"It sounds thrilling," said Frank drily.

She flashed round at him.

"You mustn't be horrid about Jasper," she said quickly; "he never speaks about you unkindly."

"I don't see why he should," said Frank, "but let's get off a subject which is – "

"Which is – what?" she challenged.

"Which is controversial," said Frank diplomatically.

She came down to the station to see him off. As he looked out of the window waving his farewells, he thought he had never seen a more lovely being or one more desirable.

It was in the afternoon of that day which saw Frank Merril speeding towards the Swiss frontier and Paris that Mr Rex Holland strode into the *Palace Hotel* at Montreux and seated himself at a table in the restaurant. The hour was late and the room was almost deserted. Giovanni, the head waiter, recognised him and came hurriedly across the room.

"Ah, M'sieur," he said, "you are back from England. I didn't expect you until the winter sports had started. Is Paris very dull?"

"I didn't come through Paris," said the other shortly; "there are many roads leading to Switzerland."

"But few pleasant roads, M'sieur. I have come to Montreux by all manner of ways, from Paris, through Pontarlier, through Ostend, Brussels, through the Hook of Holland and Amsterdam, but Paris is the only way for the man who is flying to this beautiful land."

The man at the table said nothing, scanning the menu carefully. He looked tired, as one who had taken a very long journey.

"It may interest you to know," he said after he had given his order and as Giovanni was turning away, "that I came by the longest route. Tell me, Giovanni, have you a man called Merril staying at the hotel?"

"No, M'sieur," said the other. "Is he a friend of yours?"

Mr Rex Holland smiled.

"In a sense he is a friend, in a sense he is not," he said flippantly, and offered no further enlightenment, although Giovanni waited with a deferential cock of his head.

Later, when he had finished his modest dinner, he strolled into the one long street of the town, returning to the writing room of the hotel with a number of papers which included the visitors' list, a publication printed in English and which, as it related the comings and goings of visitors not only to Lausanne, Montreux and Territet, but also to Evian and Geneva, enjoyed a fair circulation. He sat at the table and, drawing a sheet of paper from the rack, he wrote, addressed an envelope to Frank Merril, Esq., *Hôtel le France*, Geneva, slipped it into the hotel pillar box, and went to bed.

"There's a letter here for Frank," said the girl. "I wonder if it is from his agent."

She examined the envelope, which bore the Montreux postmark.

"I should imagine it is," said Saul Arthur Mann.

"Well, I am going to open it, anyway," said the girl. "Poor Frank! He will be in a state of suspense."

She tore open the envelope and took out a letter. Mr Mann saw her face go white and the letter trembled in her hand. Without a word she passed it to him and he read: "Dear Frank Merril," said the letter, "give me another month's grace, and then you may tell the whole story. – Yours, REX HOLLAND."

Saul Arthur Mann stared at the letter with open mouth.

"What does it mean?" asked the girl in a whisper.

"It means that Merril is shielding somebody," said the other; "it means – "

Suddenly his face lit up with excitement.

"The writing!" he gasped.

Her eyes followed his and for a moment she did not understand, then with a lightning sweep of her arm she snatched the letter from his hand and crumpled it in a ball.

"The writing!" said Mr Mann again. "I've seen it before. It is – Jasper Cole's!"

She looked at him steadily, though her face was white and the hand which grasped the crumpled paper was shaking.

"I think you are mistaken, Mr Mann," she said quietly.

THE MAN WHO LOOKED LIKE FRANK

Saul Arthur Mann came back to England full of his news, and found Frank at the little Jermyn Street hotel where he had installed himself, and Frank listened without interruption to the story of the letter.

"Of course," the little fellow went on, "I went straight to Montreux. The note heading was not on the paper, but I had no difficulty by comparing the qualities of papers used at the various hotels in discovering that it was written from the Palace. The head waiter knew this Rex Holland, who had been a frequent visitor, and always tipped very liberally and lived in something like style. He could not describe his patron except that he was a young man with a very languid manner who had arrived the previous morning from Holland and had immediately inquired for Frank Merril."

"From Holland! Are you sure it was the morning? I have a particular reason for asking," asked Frank quickly.

"No, it was not in the morning, now you mention it. It was in the evening. He left again the following morning by the northern train."

"How did he find my address?" asked Frank.

"Obviously from the Visitors' List. The waiter on duty in the writing-room remembered having seen him consulting the newspaper. Now, my boy, you have to be perfectly candid with me. What do you know about Rex Holland?"

Frank opened his case, took out a cigarette and lit it before he replied.

"I know what everybody knows about him," he said, with a hint of bitterness in his voice, "and something which nobody knows but me."

"But, my dear fellow," said Saul Arthur Mann, laying his hand on the other's shoulder, "surely you realise how important it is for you that you should tell me all you know."

Frank shook his head.

"The time is not come," he said, and he would make no further statement.

But on another matter he was emphatic.

"By heaven, Mann, I am not going to stand by and see May ruin her life. There's something sinister in this influence which Jasper is exercising over her. You have seen it for yourself."

Saul Arthur nodded.

"I can't understand what it is," he confessed. "Of course, Jasper is not a bad-looking fellow. He has perfect manners and is a charming companion. You don't think − ?"

"That he is winning on his merits?" Frank shook his head. "No, indeed, I do not. It is difficult for me to discuss my private affairs, and you know how reluctant I am to do so, but you are also aware of what I think of May. I was hoping that we should go back to the place where we left off, and although she is kindness itself, this girl, who is more to me than anything or anybody in the world, and who was prepared to marry me and would have married me but for Jasper's machinations, was almost cold."

He was walking up and down the room, and now halted in his stride and spread out his arms despairingly.

"What am I to do? I cannot lose her... I cannot!"

There was a fierceness in his tone which revealed the depth of his feeling, and Saul Arthur Mann understood.

"I think it is too soon to say you have lost her, Frank," he said.

He had conceived a genuine liking for Frank Merril, and the period of tribulation through which the young man had passed had heightened the respect in which he held him.

"We shall see light in dark places before we go much farther," he said. "There is something behind this crime, Frank, which I don't understand, but which I am certain is no mystery to you. I am sure that you are shielding somebody, for what reason I am not in a position to tell, but I will get to the bottom of it."

No event in the interesting life of this little man, who had spent his years in the accumulation of facts, had so distressed and piqued him as the murder of John Minute. The case had ended where the trial had left it.

Crawley, who might have offered a new aspect to the tragedy, had disappeared as completely as though the earth had swallowed him. The most strenuous efforts which the official police had made, added to the investigations which Saul Arthur Mann had conducted independently, had failed to trace the fugitive ex-sergeant of police. Obviously, he was not to be confounded with Rex Holland. He was a distinct personality, working possibly in collusion, but there the association ended.

It had occurred to the investigator that possibly Crawley had accompanied Rex Holland in his flight, but the most careful inquiries which he had pursued at Montreux were fruitless in this respect as in all others. To add to his bewilderment, investigations nearer at home were constantly bringing him across the track of Frank Merril. It was as though fate had conspired to show the boy in the blackest light. Frank had been acting as secretary to his uncle, and then Jasper Cole had suddenly appeared upon the scene from nowhere in particular. The suggestion had been made somewhat vaguely that he had come from "abroad", and it was certain that he arrived as a result of long negotiations which John Minute himself had conducted. They were negotiations which involved months of correspondence, no letter of which either from one or the other had Frank seen.

Whilst the trial was pending, the little man collected a volume of information, both from Frank and the girl, but nothing had been quite as inexplicable as this intrusion of Jasper Cole upon the scene or the extraordinary mystery which John Minute had made of his engagement.

He had written and posted all the letters to Jasper himself and had apparently received the replies, which he had burnt, at some other address of which Frank was ignorant.

Jasper had come, and then one day there had been a quarrel, not between the two young men, but between Frank and his uncle. It was a singularly bitter quarrel, and again Frank refused to discuss the cause. He left the impression upon Saul Arthur's mind that he had to some extent been responsible. And here was another fact which puzzled The Man Who Knew. Sergeant Smith, as he was then, had been to some extent responsible. It was Frank who had introduced the sergeant to Eastbourne and brought him to his uncle. But this was only one aspect of the mystery. There were others as obscure.

Saul Arthur Mann went back to his bureau, and for the twentieth time gathered the considerable dossiers he had accumulated relating to the case and to the characters, and went through them systematically and carefully.

He left his office near midnight, but at nine o'clock the next morning was on his way to Eastbourne. Constable Wiseman was, by good fortune, enjoying a day's holiday and was at work in his kitchen garden when Mr Mann's car pulled up before the cottage. Wiseman received his visitor importantly, for though the constable's prestige was regarded in official circles as having diminished as a result of the trial, it was felt by the villagers that their policeman, if he had not solved the mystery of John Minute's death, had at least gone a long way to its solution.

In the spotless room which was half kitchen and half sitting room, with its red-tiled floor covered by bright matting, Mrs Wiseman produced a well-dusted Windsor chair, which she placed at Saul Arthur Mann's disposal before she politely vanished. In a very few words the investigator stated his errand and Constable Wiseman listened in non-committal silence. When his visitor had finished, he shook his head.

"The only thing about the sergeant I know," he said, "I have already told the chief constable, who sat in that very chair," he explained; "he was always a bit of a mystery – the sergeant, I mean.

When he was 'canned', if I may use the expression, he would tell you stories by the hour, but when he was sober you couldn't get a word out of him. His daughter only lived with him for about a fortnight."

"His daughter!" said Mr Mann quickly.

"He had a daughter, as I've already notified my superiors," said Constable Wiseman gravely, "rather a pretty girl. I never saw much of her, but she was in Eastbourne off and on for about a fortnight after the sergeant came. Funny thing. I happen to know the day he arrived, because the wheel of his fly came off on my beat and I noticed the circumstances according to law and reported the same. I don't even know if she was living with him. He had a cottage down at Birlham Gap, and that is where I saw her. Yes, she was a pretty girl," he said reminiscently, "one of the slim and slender kind, very dark and with a complexion like milk. But they never found her," he said.

Again Mr Mann interrupted.

"You mean the police?"

Constable Wiseman shook his head.

"Oh, no," he said, "they've been looking for her for years, long before Mr Minute was killed."

"Who are 'they'?"

"Well, several people," said the constable slowly. "I happen to know that Mr Cole wanted to find out where she was. But then he didn't start searching until weeks after she disappeared. It is very rum," mused Constable Wiseman, "the way Mr Cole went about it. He didn't come straight to us and ask our assistance, but he had a lot of private detectives nosing around Eastbourne; one of 'em happened to be a cousin of my wife's. So we got to know about it. Cole spent a lot of money trying to trace her, and so did Mr Minute."

Saul Arthur Mann saw a faint gleam of daylight.

"Mr Minute, too?" he asked. "Was he working with Mr Cole?"

"So far as I can find out, they were both working independent of the other, Mr Cole and Mr Minute," explained Mr Wiseman; "it is what I call a mystery within a mystery, and it has never been properly cleared up. I thought something was coming out about it at the trial, but you know what a mess the lawyers made of it."

It was Constable Wiseman's firm conviction that Frank Merril had escaped through the incompetence of the Crown authorities, and there were moments in his domestic circle when he was bitter and even insubordinate on the subject.

"You still think Mr Merril was guilty?" asked Saul Arthur Mann as he took his leave of the other.

"I am as sure of it as I am that I am standing here," said the constable, not without a certain pride in the consistency of his view. "Didn't I go into the room? Wasn't he there with the deceased? Wasn't his revolver found? Hadn't there been some jiggery-pokery with his books in London?"

Saul Arthur Mann smiled.

"There are some of us who think differently, constable," he said, shaking hands with the implacable officer of the law.

He brought back to London a few new facts to be added to his record of Sergeant Crawley, alias Smith, and on these he went to work.

As has already been explained, Saul Arthur Mann had a particularly useful relationship with Scotland Yard, and fortunately, about that time, he was on the most excellent terms with official police headquarters, for he had been able to assist them in running to earth one of the most powerful blackmailing gangs that had ever operated in Europe. His files had been drawn upon to such good purpose that the police had secured convictions against the seventeen members of the gang who were in England.

He sought an interview with the Chief Commissioner, and that same night, accompanied by a small army of detectives, he made a systematic search of Silver Rents. The house into which Jasper Cole had been seen to enter was again raided, and again without result. The house was empty, save for one room, a big room which was simply furnished with a truckle-bed, a table, a chair and a lamp, and a strip of carpet. There were four rooms, two upstairs which were never used, and two on the ground floor.

At the end of a passage was a kitchen which was also empty, save for a length of bamboo ladder. From the kitchen, a bolted door led on to a tiny square of yard which was separated by three walls from yards of similar dimensions to left and right and to the back of the premises. At the back of Silver Rents was Royston Court, which was another cul-de-sac, running parallel with Silver Rents.

Mr Mann returned to the house and again searched the upstairs rooms, looking particularly for a trap door; for the bamboo ladder suggested some such exit. This time, however, he completely failed. Jasper Cole, he found, had made only one visit to the house since Mr Minute's death. It is a curious fact, as showing the localising of interest, that Silver Rents knew nothing of what had occurred almost at its doors, and though it had at its fingertips all the gossip of the docks and the Thames Iron Works, if was profoundly ignorant of what was common property in Royston Court. It is even more remarkable that Saul Arthur Mann with his squadron of detectives should have confined their investigations to Silver Rents.

The investigator was baffled and disappointed, but by the oddest of chances he was to pick up yet another thread of the Minute mystery, a thread which, however, was to lead him into an even deeper maze than that which he had already and so unsuccessfully attempted to penetrate.

Three days after his search of Silver Rents, business took Mr Mann to Camden Town. To be exact, he had gone at the request of the police to Holloway Gaol to see a prisoner who had turned State's evidence on a matter in which the police and Mr Mann were equally interested. Very foolishly, he had dismissed his taxi, and when he emerged from the doors there was no conveyance in sight. He decided rather than take the trams, which would have carried him to King's Cross, to walk, and, since he hated main roads, he had taken a short cut which, as he knew, would lead him into the Hampstead Road.

Thus he found himself in Flowerton Road, a thoroughfare of respectable detached houses occupied by the superior industrial type. He was striding along, swinging his umbrella and humming, as was his wont, an unmusical rendering of a popular tune, when his attention was attracted to a sight which took his breath away and brought him to a halt.

It was half-past five and dull, but his eyesight was excellent and it was impossible for him to make a mistake. The houses of Flowerton Road stand back and are separated from the sidewalk by diminutive gardens. The front doors are approached by six or seven steps, and it was on the top of one of these flights, in front of an open door, that the scene was enacted which brought Mr Mann to a standstill.

The characters were a young man and girl. The girl was extremely pretty and very pale. The man was the exact double of Frank Merril. He was dressed in a rough tweed suit and wore a soft felt hat with a fairly wide brim. But it was not the appearance of this remarkable apparition which startled the investigator. It was the attitude of the two people. The girl was evidently pleading with her companion. Saul Arthur Mann was too far away to hear what she said, but he saw the young man shake himself loose from the girl. She again grasped his arm and raised her face imploringly.

Mr Mann gasped, for he saw the young man's hand come up and strike her back into the house. Then he caught hold of the door and banged it savagely, walked down the stairs and, turning, hurried away.

The investigator stood as though he were rooted to the spot, and before he could recover himself the fellow had turned the corner of the road and was out of sight. Saul Arthur Mann took off his hat and wiped his forehead. All his initiative was for the moment paralysed. He walked slowly up to the gate and hesitated. What excuse could he have for calling? If this were Frank, assuredly his own views were all wrong and the mystery was a greater mystery still.

His energies began to reawaken. He took a note of the number of the house and hurried off after the young man. When he turned the corner, his quarry had vanished. He hurried to the next corner, but without overtaking the object of his pursuit. Fortunately, at this moment, he found an empty taxi cab and hailed it.

"Grimm's Hotel, Jermyn Street," he directed.

At least he could satisfy his mind upon one point.

A LETTER IN THE GRATE

Grimm's Hotel is in reality a block of flats with a restaurant attached. The restaurant is little more than a kitchen from whence meals are served to residents in their rooms. Frank's suite was on the third floor, and Mr Mann, paying his cabman, hurried into the hall, stepped into the automatic lift, pressed the button and was deposited at Frank's door. He knocked with a sickening sense of apprehension that there would be no answer. To his delight and amazement, he heard Frank's firm step in the tiny hall of his flat and the door was opened. Frank was in the act of dressing for dinner.

"Come in, SAM," he said cheerily, "and tell me all the news." He led the way back to his room and resumed the delicate operation of tying his dress bow.

"How long have you been here?" asked Mr Mann.

Frank looked at him inquiringly.

"How long have I been here?" he repeated. "I cannot tell you the exact time, but I have been here since a short while after lunch."

Mr Mann was bewildered and still unconvinced.

"What clothes did you take off?"

It was Frank's turn to look amazed.

"Clothes?" he repeated. "What are you driving at, my dear chap?"

"What suit were you wearing today?" persisted Saul Arthur Mann.

Frank disappeared into his dressing room and came out with a tumbled bundle which he dropped on a chair. It was the blue suit which he usually affected.

"Now what is the joke?"

"It is no joke," said the other. "I could have sworn that I saw you less than half an hour ago in Camden Town."

"I won't pretend that I don't know where Camden Town is," smiled Frank, "but I have not visited that interesting locality for many years."

Saul Arthur Mann was silent. It was obvious to him that whoever was the occupant of 69 Flowerton Road, it was not Frank Merril. Frank listened to the narrative with interest.

"You were probably mistaken – the light played you a trick, I expect," he said.

But Mr Mann was emphatic.

"I could have taken an oath in a court that it was you," he said.

Frank stared out of the window.

"How very curious!" he mused. "I suppose I cannot very well prosecute a man for looking like me – poor girl!"

"Of whom are you thinking?" asked the other.

"I was thinking of the unfortunate woman," answered Frank. "What brutes there are in the world!"

"You gave me a terrible fright," admitted his friend.

Frank's laugh was loud and hearty.

"I suppose you saw me figuring in a court, charged with common assault," he said.

"I saw more than that," said the other gravely, "and I see more than that now. Suppose you have a double, and suppose that double is working in collusion with your enemies."

Frank shook his head wearily.

"My dear friend," he said with a little smile, "I am tired of supposing things. Come and dine with me."

But Mr Mann had another engagement. Moreover, he wanted to think things out.

Thinking things out was a process which brought little reward in this instance, and he went to bed that night a vexed and puzzled man. He always had his breakfast in bed at ten o'clock in the morning, for he had reached the age of habits, and had fixed ten o'clock, since it gave his clerks time to bring down his personal mail from the office to his private residence.

It was a profitable mail, it was an exciting mail, and it contained an element of rich promise, for it included a letter from Constable Wiseman.

DEAR SIR,

Re our previous conversation I have just come across one of the photographs of the young lady (Sergeant Smith's daughter). It was given to the private detective who was searching for her. It was given to my wife by her cousin and I send it to you, hoping it may be of some use.

Yours respectfully,
PETER JOHN WISEMAN.

The photograph was wrapped in a piece of tissue paper and Saul Arthur Mann opened it eagerly. He looked at the oblong card and gasped, for the girl who was depicted there was the girl he had seen on the steps of 69 Flowerton Road.

A telephone message prepared Frank for the news, and an hour later the two men were together in the office of the bureau.

"I am going along to that house to see the girl," said Saul Arthur Mann. "Will you come?"

"With all the pleasure in life," said Frank. "Curiously enough, I am as eager to find her as you. I remember her very well, and one of the quarrels I had with my uncle was due to her. She had come up to the house on behalf of her father, and I thought uncle treated her rather brutally."

("Point number one cleared up," thought Saul Arthur Mann.)

"Then she disappeared," Frank went on, "and Jasper came on the scene. There was some association between this girl and Jasper, which I have never been able to fathom. All I know is that he took a tremendous interest in her and tried to find her, and, so far as I remember, he never succeeded."

Mr Mann's car was at the door, and in a few minutes they were deposited before the prim exterior of Number 69.

The door was opened by a girl servant who stared from Saul Arthur Mann to his companion.

"There is a lady living here," said Mr Mann.

He produced the photograph.

"This is the lady."

The girl nodded, still staring at Frank.

"I want to see her."

"She's gone," said the girl.

"You are looking at me very intently," said Frank. "Have you ever seen me before?"

"Yes, sir," said the girl, "you used to come here, or a gentleman very much like you – you are Mr Merril."

"That is my name," smiled Frank, "but I do not think I have ever been here before."

"Where has the lady gone?" asked Saul Arthur.

"She went last night. Took all her boxes and went off in a cab."

"Is anybody living in the house?"

"No, sir," said the girl.

"How long have you been in service here?"

"About a week, sir," replied the girl.

"We are friends of hers," said Saul Arthur shamelessly, "and we have been asked to call to see if everything is all right."

The girl hesitated, but Saul Arthur Mann, with that air of authority which he so readily assumed, swept past her and began an inspection of the house.

It was plainly furnished, but the furniture was good.

"Apparently the spurious Mr Merril had plenty of money," said Saul Arthur Mann.

There were no photographs or papers visible until they came to the bedroom, where in the grate was a torn sheet of paper bearing a few lines of fine writing which Mr Mann immediately annexed.

Before they left, Frank again asked the girl: "Was the gentleman who lived here really like me?"

"Yes, sir," said the little slavey.

"Have a good look at me," said Frank humorously, and the girl glared again.

"Something like you," she admitted.

"Did he talk like me?"

"I never heard him talk, sir," said the girl.

"Tell me," said Saul Arthur Mann, "was he kind to his wife?"

A faint grin appeared on the face of the little servant.

"They are always rowing," she admitted; "a bullying fellow he was, and she was frightened of him. Are you the police?" she asked with sudden interest.

Frank shook his head.

"No, we are not the police."

He gave the girl half a crown and walked down the steps ahead of his companion.

"It is rather awkward if I have a double who bullies his wife and lives in Camden Town," he said as the car hummed back to the city office.

Saul Arthur Mann was silent during the journey and only answered in monosyllables.

Again in the privacy of his office he took the torn letter and carefully pieced it together on his desk. It bore no address and there were no affectionate preliminaries: "You must get out of London" (it ran); "Saul Arthur Mann saw you both today. Go to the old place and await instructions."

There was no signature, but across the table the two men looked at one another, for the writing was the writing of Jasper Cole.

THE COMING OF SERGEANT SMITH

Jasper Cole at that moment was trudging through the snow to the little chalet which May Nuttall had taken on the slope of the mountain overlooking Chamonix. The sleigh which had brought them up from the station was at the foot of the rise. May saw him from the verandah and coo-eed a welcome. He stamped the snow from his boots and ran up the steps of the verandah to meet her.

"This is a very pleasant surprise," she said, giving him both her hands and looking at him approvingly. He had lost much of his pallor and his face was tanned and healthy, though a little fine-drawn.

"It was rather a mad thing to do, wasn't it?" he confessed ruefully.

"You are such a confirmed bachelor, Jasper, that I believe you hate doing anything outside your regular routine. Why did you come all the way from Holland to the Haute Savoie?"

He had followed her into the warm and cosy sitting room and was warming his chilled fingers by the big log fire which burned on the hearth.

"Can you ask? I came to see you."

"And how are all the experiments going?"

She turned him to another topic in some hurry.

"There have been no experiments since last month – at least, not the kind of experiments you mean. The one in which I have been engaged has been very successful."

"And what was that?" she asked curiously.

"I will tell you one of these days," he said.

He was staying at the Hôtel des Alpes and hoped to be a week in Chamonix. They chatted about the weather, the early snow which had covered the valley in a mantle of white, and the tantalizing behaviour of Mont Blanc, which had not been visible since May had arrived, of the early avalanches which awakened her with their thunder on the night of her arrival, of the pleasant road to Argentières, of the villages by the Col de Balme which was buried in snow, of the sparkling, ethereal green of the great glacier – of everything save that which was nearest to their thoughts and to their hearts.

Jasper broke the ice when he referred to Frank's visit to Geneva.

"How did you know?" she asked, suddenly grave.

"Somebody told me," he said casually.

"Jasper, were you ever at Montreux?" she asked, looking him straight in the eye.

"I have been to Montreux, or rather to Caux," he said, "that is the village on the mountain above and one has to go through Montreux to reach it. Why did you ask?"

A sudden chill had fallen upon her, which she did not shake off that day or the next.

They made the usual excursions together, climbed up the wooded slopes of the Butte, and on the third morning after his arrival stood together in the clear dawn and watched the first pink rays of the sun striking the humped summit of Mont Blanc.

"Isn't it glorious?" she whispered.

He nodded.

The serene beauty of it all, the purity, the majestic aloofness of the mountains, at once depressed and exalted her, brought her nearer to the sublimity of ancient truths, cleansed her of petty fears. She turned to him unexpectedly and asked: "Jasper, who killed John Minute?"

He made no reply. His wistful eyes were fixed hungrily upon the glories of light and shade, of space, of inaccessibility, of purity, of colouring, of all that dawn upon Mont Blanc comprehended. When he spoke, his voice was lowered to almost a whisper.

"I know that the man who killed John Minute is alive and free," he said.

"Who was he?"

"If you do not know now, you may never know," he said.

There was a silence which lasted for fully five minutes, and the crimson light upon the mountain top had paled to lemon yellow.

Then she asked again: "Are you directly or indirectly guilty?"

He shook his head.

"Neither directly nor indirectly," he said shortly, and the next minute she was in his arms.

There had been no word of love between them, no tender passage, no letter which the world could not read. It was a lovemaking which had begun where other lovemakings end – in conquest and in surrender. In this strange way, beyond all understanding, May Nuttall became engaged and announced the fact in the briefest of letters to her friends.

A fortnight later the girl arrived in England and was met at Charing Cross by Saul Arthur Mann. She was radiantly happy and bubbling over with good spirits, a picture of health and beauty.

All this Mr Mann observed with a sinking heart. He had a duty to perform, and that duty was not a pleasant one. He knew it was useless to reason with the girl. He could offer her no more than half-formed theories and suspicions, but at least he had one trump card. He debated in his mind whether he should play this, for here, too, his information was of the scantiest description. He carried his account of the girl to Frank Merril.

"My dear Frank, she is simply infatuated," said the little man in despair. "Oh, if that infernal record of mine was only completed, I could convince her in a second! There is no single investigation I have ever undertaken which has been so disappointing."

"Can nothing be done?" asked Frank. "I cannot believe that it will happen. Marry Jasper! Good God! – after all – "

His voice was hoarse – the hand he raised in protest shook.

Saul Arthur Mann scratched his chin.

"Suppose you saw her," he suggested, and added a little grimly: "I will see Mr Cole at the same time."

Frank hesitated.

"I can understand your reluctance," the little man went on, "but there is too much at stake to allow your finer feelings to stop you. This matter has got to be prevented at all costs. We are fighting for time. In a month, possibly less, we may have the whole of the facts in our hands."

"Have you found out anything about the girl in Camden Town?" asked Frank.

"She has disappeared completely," replied the other; "every clue we have had has led nowhere."

Frank dressed himself with unusual care that afternoon, and having previously telephoned and secured the girl's permission to call, he presented himself to the minute. She was, as usual, cordiality itself.

"I was rather hurt at your not calling before, Frank," she said. "You have come to congratulate me?"

She looked at him straight in the eyes as she said this.

"You can hardly expect that, May," he said gently, "knowing how much you are to me and how greatly I wanted you. Honestly I cannot understand it, and I can only suppose that you, whom I love better than anything in the world, and you mean more to me than any other human being, share the suspicion which surrounds me like a poison cloud."

"Yet if I shared that suspicion," she said calmly, "would I let you see me? No, Frank, I was a child when – you know. It was only a few months ago, but I believe, indeed I know, it would have been the greatest mistake I could possibly have made: I should have been a very unhappy woman, for I have loved Jasper all along."

She said this evenly, without any display of emotion or embarrassment. Frank, narrating the interview to Saul Arthur Mann, described the speech as almost mechanical.

"I hope you are going to take it nicely," she went on, "that we are going to be such good friends as we always were, and that even the memory of your poor uncle's death and the ghastly trial which followed and the part that Jasper played will not spoil our good friendship."

"But don't you see what it means to me?" he burst forth, and for a second they looked at one another, and Frank divined her thoughts and winced.

"I know what you are thinking," he said huskily. "You are thinking of all the beastly things that were said at the trial, that if I had gained you, I should have gained all that I tried to gain."

She went red.

"It was horrid of me, wasn't it?" she confessed, "and yet that idea came to me. One cannot control one's thoughts, Frank, and you must be content to know that I believe in your innocence. There are some thoughts which flourish in one's mind like weeds and which refuse to be uprooted. Don't blame me if I recalled the lawyer's words; it was an involuntary, hateful thought."

He inclined his head.

"There is another which is not involuntary," she went on, "and it is because I want to retain our friendship and I want everything to go on as usual that I am asking you one question. Your twenty-fourth birthday has come and gone – you told me that your uncle's design was to keep you unmarried until that day. You are still unmarried and your twenty-fourth birthday has passed. What has happened?"

"Many things have happened," he replied quietly. "My uncle is dead. I am a rich man apart from the accident of his legacy. I could meet you on level terms."

"I knew nothing of this," she said quickly.

He shrugged his shoulders.

"Didn't Jasper tell you?" he asked.

"No; Jasper told me nothing."

Frank drew a long breath.

"Then I can only say that until the mystery of my uncle's death is solved, you cannot know," he said. "I can only repeat what I have already told you."

She offered her hand.

"I believe you, Frank," she said, "and I was wrong even to doubt you in the smallest degree."

He took her hand and held it.

"May," he said, "what is this strange fascination that Jasper has over you?"

For the second time in that interview she flushed and pulled her hand back.

"There is nothing unusual in the fascination which Jasper exercises," she smiled quickly, recovering almost against her will from the little twinge of anger she felt; "it is the influence which every woman has felt and which you one day will feel."

He laughed bitterly.

"Then nothing will make you change your mind?" he said.

"Nothing in the world," she answered emphatically.

For a moment she was sorry for him as he stood, both hands resting on a chair, his eyes on the ground, a picture of despair, and she crossed to him and slipped her arm through his.

"Don't take it so badly, Frank," she said softly. "I am a capricious, foolish girl, I know, and I am really not worth a moment's suffering."

He shook himself together, gathered up his hat, his stick and his overcoat, and offered his hand.

"Goodbye," he said, "and good luck!"

In the meantime another interview of a widely different character was taking place in the little house which Jasper Cole occupied on the Portsmouth Road. Jasper and Saul Arthur Mann had met before, but this was the first visit that the investigator had paid to the home of John Minute's heir.

Jasper was waiting at the door to greet the little man when he arrived, and had offered him a quiet but warm welcome and led the way to the beautiful study, which was half laboratory, which he had built for himself since John Minute's death.

"I am coming straight to the point without any beating about the bush, Mr Cole," said the little man, depositing his bag on the side of his chair and opening it with a jerk. "I will tell you frankly that I am acting on Mr Merril's behalf and that I am also acting, as I believe, in the interests of justice."

"Your motives at any rate are admirable," said Jasper, pushing back the papers which littered his library table, and seating himself on the edge.

"You are probably aware that you are to some extent under suspicion, Mr Cole."

"Under your suspicion or the suspicion of the authorities?" asked the other coolly.

"Under mine," said Saul Arthur Mann emphatically. "I cannot speak for the authorities."

"In what direction does this suspicion run?"

He thrust his hands deep in his trousers pockets and eyed the other keenly.

"My first suspicion is that you are well aware as to who murdered John Minute."

Jasper Cole nodded.

"I am perfectly aware that he was murdered by your friend, Mr Merril," he said.

"I suggest," said Saul Arthur Mann calmly, "that you know the murderer, and you know the murderer was *not* Frank Merril."

Jasper made no reply and a faint smile flickered for a second at the corner of his mouth, but he gave no other sign of his inward feelings.

"And the other point you wish to raise?" he asked.

"The other is a more delicate subject, since it involves a lady," said the little man. "You are about to be married to Miss Nuttall."

Jasper Cole nodded.

"You have obtained an extraordinary influence over the lady in the past few months."

"I hope so!" said the other cheerfully.

"It is an influence which might have been brought about by normal methods, but it is also one" – Saul Arthur leant over and tapped the table emphatically with each word – "which might be secured by a very clever chemist who had found a way of sapping the will of his victim."

"By the administration of drugs?" asked Jasper.

"By the administration of drugs," repeated Saul Arthur Mann.

Jasper Cole smiled.

"I should like to know the drug," he said; "one would make a fortune, to say nothing of benefiting humanity to an extraordinary degree by its employment. For example, I might give you a dose and you would tell me all that you know – I am told that your knowledge is fairly extensive," he bantered. "Surely you, Mr Mann, with your remarkable collection of information on all subjects under the sun, do not suggest that such a drug exists?"

"On the contrary," said The Man Who Knew in triumph, "it is known and is employed. It was known as long ago as the days of the Borgias. It was employed in France in the days of Louis Sixteenth. It has been to some extent rediscovered and used in lunatic asylums to quieten dangerous patients."

He saw the interest deepen in the other's eyes.

"I have never heard of that," said Jasper slowly; "the only drug that is employed for that purpose is, as far as I know, bromide of potassium."

Mr Mann produced a slip of paper and read off a list of names, mostly of mental institutions in USA and in Germany.

"Oh, that drug!" said Jasper Cole contemptuously. "I know the use to which that is put. There was an article on the subject in the *British Medical Journal* three months ago. It is a modified kind of 'Twilight sleep,' hyoscine and morphia. I'm afraid, Mr Mann," he went on, "you have come on a fruitless errand, and speaking as a humble student of science, I may suggest without offence that your theories are wholly fantastic."

"Then I will put another suggestion to you, Mr Cole," said the little man without resentment, "and to me this constitutes the chief reason why you should not marry the lady whose confidence I enjoy and who, I feel sure, will be influenced by my advice."

"And what is that?" asked Jasper.

"It affects your own character, and it is in consequence a very embarrassing matter for me to discuss," said the little man.

Again the other favoured him with that inscrutable smile of his.

"My moral character, I presume, is now being assailed," he said flippantly. "Please go on – you promise to be interesting."

"You were in Holland a short time ago. Does Miss Nuttall know this?"

Jasper nodded.

"She is well aware of the fact."

"You were in Holland with a lady," accused Mr Mann slowly. "Is Miss Nuttall well aware of this fact, too?"

Jasper slipped from the table and stood upright. Through his narrow lids he looked down upon his accuser.

"Is that all you know?" he asked softly.

"Not all, but one of the things I know," retorted the other. "You were seen in her company. She was staying in the same hotel with you as 'Mrs Cole'."

Jasper nodded.

"You will excuse me if I decline to discuss the matter," he said.

"Suppose I ask Miss Nuttall to discuss it?" challenged the little man.

"You are the master of your own actions," said Jasper Cole quickly, "and I dare say if you regard it as expedient, you will tell her; but I can promise you that whether you tell her or not, I shall marry Miss Nuttall."

With this he ushered his visitor to the door, and hardly waited for the car to drive off before he had shut that door behind him.

Late that night the two friends foregathered and exchanged their experiences.

"I am sure there is something very wrong indeed," said Frank emphatically. "She was not herself. She spoke mechanically, almost as though she were reciting a lesson. You had the feeling that she was connected by wires with somebody who was dictating her every word and action. It is damnable, Mann. What can we do?"

"We must prevent the marriage," said the little man quietly, "and employ every means that opportunity suggests to that purpose. Make no mistake," he said emphatically. "Cole will stop at nothing. His attitude was one big bluff. He knows that I have beaten him. It was only by luck that I found out about the woman in Holland. I got my agent to examine the hotel register, and there it was, without any attempt at disguise: 'Mr and Mrs Cole of London'."

"The thing to do is to see May at once," said Frank, "and put all the facts before her, though I hate the idea – it seems like sneaking."

"Sneaking!" exploded Saul Arthur Mann. "What nonsense you talk! You are too full of scruples, my friend, for this work. I will see her tomorrow."

"I will go with you," said Frank, after a moment's thought. "I have no wish to escape my responsibility in the matter. She will probably hate me for my interference, but I have reached beyond the point whether I care – so long as she can be saved."

It was agreed that they should meet one another at the office in the morning and make their way together.

"Remember this," said Mann seriously, before they parted, "that if Cole finds the game is up, he will stop at nothing."

"Do you think we ought to take precautions?" asked Frank.

"Honestly, I do," confessed the other. "I don't think we can get the men from the Yard, but there is a very excellent agency which sometimes works for me and they can provide a guard for the girl."

"I wish you would get in touch with them," said Frank earnestly. "I am worried sick over this business. She ought never to be left out of their sight. I will see if I can have a talk to her maid, so that we may know whenever she is going out. There ought to be a man on a motorcycle always waiting about the Savoy to follow her wherever she goes."

They parted at the entrance of the bureau, Saul Arthur Mann returning to telephone the necessary instructions. How necessary they were was proved that very night.

At nine o'clock May was sitting down to a solitary dinner when a telegram was delivered to her. It was from the chief of the little mission in which she had been interested, and ran: "Very urgent. Have something of the greatest importance to tell you." It was signed with the name of the matron of the mission, and leaving her dinner untouched, May only delayed long enough to change her dress before she was speeding in a taxi eastward.

She arrived at the "hall," which was the headquarters of the mission, to find it in darkness. A man who was evidently a new helper was waiting in the doorway and addressed her.

"You are Miss Nuttall, aren't you? I thought so. The matron has gone down to Silver Rents, and she asked me to go along with you."

The girl dismissed the taxi and in company with her guide threaded the narrow tangle of streets between the mission and Silver Rents. She was halfway along one of the ill-lighted thoroughfares when she noticed that drawn up by the side of the road was a big, handsome motorcar, and she wondered what had brought this evidence of luxurious living to the mean streets of Canning Town. She was not left in doubt very long, for as she came up to the lights and was shielding her eyes from their glare her arms were tightly grasped, a shawl was thrown over her head and she was lifted and thrust into the car's interior. A hand gripped her throat.

"You scream and I will kill you," hissed a voice in her ear.

At that moment the car started, and the girl with a scream which was strangled in her throat fell swooning back on her seat.

May recovered consciousness to find the car still rushing forward in the dark and the hand of her captor still resting at her throat.

"You are a sensible girl," said a muffled voice, "and do as you're told and no harm will come to you."

It was too dark to see his face, and it was evident that even if there were light, the face was so well concealed that she could not recognise the speaker. Then she remembered that this man, who had acted as her guide, had been careful to keep in the shadow of whatever light there was whilst he was conducting her, as he said, to the matron.

"Where are you taking me?" she asked.

"You'll know in time," was the non-committal answer.

It was a wild night; rain splashed against the windows of the car and she could hear the wind howling above the noise of the engines. They were evidently going into the country, for now and again by the light of the headlamps she glimpsed hedges and trees which flashed past. Her captor suddenly let down one of the windows and leant out, giving some instructions to the driver. What they were she guessed, for the lights were suddenly switched off and the car ran in darkness.

The girl was in a panic for all her bold showing. She knew that this desperate man was fearless of consequence, and that, if her death would achieve his ends and the ends of his partners, her life was in imminent peril. What were those ends, she wondered? Were these the same men who had done to death John Minute?

"Who are you?" she asked.

There was a little chuckling laugh.

"You'll know soon enough."

The words were hardly out of his mouth when there was a terrific crash. The car stopped suddenly and canted over and the girl was jerked forward to her knees. Every pane of glass in the car was smashed, and it was clear from the angle it lay that irredeemable damage had been done. The man scrambled up, and kicked open the door and jumped out.

"Level crossing gate, sir," said the voice of the chauffeur. "I've broken my wrist."

With the disappearance of her captor the girl had felt for the fastening of the opposite door and had turned it. To her delight if opened smoothly and had evidently been unaffected by the jam. She stepped out to the road, trembling in every limb.

She felt rather than saw the level crossing gate, and knew that at one side was a swing gate for passengers. She reached this when her abductor discovered her flight.

"Come back!" he cried hoarsely.

She heard a roar and saw a flashing of lights and fled across the line just as an express train came flying northward. It missed her by inches, and the force of the wind threw her to the ground. She scrambled up, tumbled across the remaining rails and, reaching the gate opposite, fled down the dark road. She had gained just that much time which the train took in passing. She ran blindly along the dark road, slipping and stumbling in the mud, and she heard her pursuer squelching through the mud in the rear.

The wind blew her hair awry, the rain beat down upon her face, but she stumbled on. Suddenly she slipped and fell, and as she struggled to her feet the heavy hand of her pursuer fell upon her shoulder and she screamed aloud.

"None of that," said the voice, and his hand covered her mouth.

At that moment a bright light enveloped the two, a light so intensely, dazzlingly white, so unexpected, that it hit the girl almost like a blow. It came from somewhere not two yards away, and the man released his hold upon the girl and stared at the light.

"Hullo!" said a voice from the darkness. "What's the game?"

She was behind the man and could not see his face. All that she knew was that here was help, unexpected, heaven-sent, and she strove to recover her breath and her speech.

"It is all right," growled the man, "She's a lunatic and I'm taking her to the asylum."

Suddenly the light was pushed forward to the man's face, and a heavy hand was laid upon his shoulder.

"You are, are you?" said the other. "Well, I am going to take you to a lunatic asylum, Sergeant Smith, or Crawley, or whatever your name is. You know me – my name's Wiseman."

For a moment the man stood as though petrified, and then with a sudden jerk he wrenched his hand free and sprang at the policeman with a wild yell of rage, and in a second both men were rolling over in the darkness. Constable Wiseman was no child, but he had lost his initial advantage, and by the time he got to his feet and had found his electric torch Crawley had vanished.

THE MAN CALLED "MERRIL"

"If Wiseman did not think you were a murderer, I should regard him as an intelligent being," said Saul Arthur Mann.

"Have they found Crawley?" asked Frank.

"No, he got away. The chauffeur and the car were hired from a West End garage, with this story of a lunatic who had to be removed to an asylum, and, apparently, Crawley, or Smith, was the man who hired them. He even paid a little extra for the damage which the alleged lunatic might do to the car. The chauffeur says that he had some doubt, and had intended to inform the police after he had arrived at his destination. As a matter of fact, they were just outside Eastbourne when the accident occurred. Where did he say he was taking her?" he asked Frank.

"He was told to drive into Eastbourne, where more detailed instructions would be given to him. The police have confirmed his story and he has been released. I have just come from May," said Frank; "she looks none the worse for her exciting adventure. I hope you have arranged to have her guarded?"

Saul Arthur Mann nodded.

"It will be the last adventure of that kind our friend will attempt," he said.

"Still, this enlightens us a little. We know that Mr Rex Holland has an accomplice, and that that accomplice is Sergeant Smith, so we may presume that they were both in the murder. Constable Wiseman has been suitably rewarded, as he well deserves," said Frank heartily.

"You bear no malice?" smiled Saul Arthur Mann.

Frank laughed and shook his head.

"How can one?" he asked simply.

May had another visitor. Jasper Cole came hurriedly to London at the first intimation of the outrage, but was reassured by the girl's appearance.

"It was awfully thrilling," she said; "but really, I am not greatly distressed – in fact, I think I look less tired than you."

He nodded.

"That is very possible. I did not go to bed until very late this morning," he said. "I was so engrossed in my research work that I did not realise it was morning until they brought me my tea."

"You haven't been in bed all night?" she said, shocked, and shook her head reprovingly. "That is one of your habits of life which will have to be changed," she warned him.

Jasper Cole did not dismiss her unpleasant experience as lightly as she.

"I wonder what the object of it all was?" he said, "and why they took you back to Eastbourne? I think we shall find that the headquarters of this infernal combination is somewhere in Sussex."

"Mr Mann doesn't think so," she said, "but believes that the car was to be met by another at Eastbourne and I was to be transferred. He says that the whole business of taking me there was to throw the police off the scent."

She shivered.

"It wasn't a nice experience," she confessed.

The interview took place in the afternoon, and was some two hours after Frank had interviewed the girl – Saul Arthur Mann had gone to Eastbourne to bring her back. Jasper had arranged to spend the night in town and had booked two stalls at the Hippodrome. She had told Saul Arthur Mann this, in accordance with her promise to keep him informed as to her movements, and she was therefore surprised when, half an hour later, the little investigator presented himself.

She met him in the presence of her fiancé, and it was clear to Jasper what Saul Arthur Mann's intentions were.

"I don't want to make myself a nuisance," he said, "but before we go any farther, Miss Nuttall, there are certain matters on which you ought to be informed. I have every reason to believe that I know who was responsible for the outrage of last night and I do not intend risking a repetition."

"Who do you think was responsible?" asked the girl quietly.

"I honestly believe that the author is in this room," was the startling response.

"You mean me?" asked Jasper Cole angrily.

"I mean you, Mr Cole. I believe that you are the man who planned the coup and that you are its sole author," said the other.

The girl stared at him in astonishment.

"You surely do not mean what you say."

"I mean that Mr Cole has every reason for wishing to marry you," he said. "What that reason is, I do not know completely, but I shall discover. I am satisfied," he went on slowly, "that Mr Cole is already married."

She looked from one to the other.

"Already married?" repeated Jasper.

"If he is not already married," said Saul Arthur Mann bluntly, "then I have been indiscreet. The only thing I can tell you is that your fiancé has been travelling on the Continent with a lady who describes herself as Mrs Cole."

Jasper said nothing for a moment, but looked at the other oddly and thoughtfully.

"I understand, Mr Mann," he said at length, "that you collect the facts as other people collect postage stamps?"

Saul Arthur Mann bristled.

"You may carry this off, sir, if you can – "

"Let me speak," said Jasper Cole, raising his voice. "I want to ask you this. Have you a complete record of John Minute's life?"

"I know it so well," said Saul Arthur Mann emphatically, "that I could repeat his history word for word."

"Will you sit down, May?" said Jasper, taking the girl's hand in his and gently forcing her to a chair. "We are going to put Mr Mann's memory to the test."

"Do you seriously mean that you want me to repeat that history?" asked the other suspiciously.

"I mean just that," said Jasper, and drew up a chair for his unpleasant visitor.

The record of John Minute's life came trippingly from Mann's tongue. He knew to an extraordinary extent the details of that strange and wild career.

"In 1892," said the investigator, continuing his narrative, "he was married at St Bride's Church, Port Elizabeth, to Agnes Gertrude Cole."

"Cole," murmured Jasper.

The little man looked at him with open mouth.

"Cole! Good Lord – you are – "

"I am his son," said Jasper quietly. "I am one of his two children. Your information is that there was one. As a matter of fact, there were two. My mother left my father with one of the greatest scoundrels that has ever lived. He took her to Australia, where my sister was born six months after she had left John Minute. There her friend deserted her, and she worked for seven years as a kitchen-maid in Melbourne, in order to save enough money to bring us to Cape Town. My mother opened a tea shop off Adderley Street and earned enough to educate me and my sister. It was there she met Crawley, and Crawley promised to use his influence with my father to bring about a reconciliation for her children's sake. I do not know what was the result of his attempt, but I gather it was unsuccessful, and things went on very much as they were before.

"Then, one day, when I was still at the South African College, my mother went home, taking my sister with her. I have reason to believe that Crawley was responsible for her sailing and that he met them on landing. All that I knew was that from that day my mother disappeared. She had left me a sum of money to continue my studies, but after eight months had passed and no word had come from her, I decided to go on to England. I have since learnt what had happened. My mother had been seized with a stroke and had been conveyed to the workhouse infirmary by Crawley, who had left her there and had taken my sister, who, apparently, he passed off as his own daughter.

"I did not know this at the time, but being well aware of my father's identity, I wrote to him asking him for help to discover my mother. He answered, telling me that my mother was dead, that Crawley had told him so, and that there was no trace of Marguerite, my sister. We exchanged a good many letters, and then my father asked me to come and act as his secretary and assist him in his search for Marguerite. What he did not know was that Crawley's alleged daughter, whom he had not seen, was the girl for whom he was seeking. I fell into the new life and found John Minute – I can scarcely call him 'father' – much more bearable than I expected; and then one day I found my mother."

"You found your mother?" said Saul Arthur Mann, a light dawning upon him.

"Your persistent search of the little house in Silver Rents produced nothing," he smiled. "Had you taken the bamboo ladder and crossed the yard at the back of the house, into another yard, and through the door, you would have come to Number 16 Royston Court, and you would have been considerably surprised to find an interior much more luxurious than you would have expected in that quarter. In Royston Court, they spoke of Number 16 as 'the house with the nurses', because there were always three nurses on duty, and nobody ever saw the inside of the house but themselves. There you would have found my mother, bedridden, and, indeed, so ill that the doctors who saw her would not allow her to be moved from the house.

"I furnished this hovel piece by piece, generally at night, because I did not want to excite the curiosity of the people in the Court, nor did I wish this matter to reach the ears of John Minute. I felt that whilst I retained his friendship and his confidence there was at least a chance of his reconciliation with my mother, and that before all things she desired. It was not to be," he said sadly. "John Minute was struck down at the moment my plans seemed as though they were going to result in complete success. Strangely enough, with his death my mother made an extraordinary recovery and I was able to move her to the Continent. She had always wanted to see Holland and France, and at this moment" – he turned to the girl with a smile –"she is in the chalet which you occupied during your holiday."

Mr Mann was dumbfounded. All his pet theories had gone by the board.

"But what of your sister?" he asked at last.

A black look gathered in Jasper Cole's face.

"My sister's whereabouts are known to me now," he said shortly. "For some time she lived in Camden Town at Number 69 Flowerton Road. At the present moment she is nearer and is watched night and day, almost as carefully as Mr Mann's agents are watching you." He smiled again at the girl.

"Watching me?" she said, startled.

Saul Arthur Mann went red.

"It was my idea," he said stiffly.

"And a very excellent one," agreed Jasper, "but unfortunately, you appointed your guards too late."

Mr Mann went back to his office, his brain in a whirl, yet such was his habit that he did not allow himself to speculate upon the new and amazing situation until he had carefully jotted down every new fact he had collected.

It was astounding that he had overlooked the connection between Jasper Cole and John Minute's wife. His labours did not cease until eleven o'clock, and he was preparing to go home, when the commissionaire who acted as caretaker came to tell him that a lady wished to see him.

"A lady? At this hour of the night?" said Mr Mann, perturbed. "Tell her to come in the morning."

"I have told her that, sir, but she insists upon seeing you tonight."

"What is her name?"

"Mrs Merril," said the commissionaire.

Saul Arthur Mann collapsed into his chair.

"Show her up," he said feebly.

He had no difficulty in recognising the girl, who came timidly into the room, as the original of the photograph which had been sent to him by Constable Wiseman. She was plainly dressed and wore no ornament, and she was undeniably pretty, but there was about her a furtiveness and nervous indecision which spoke of her apprehension.

"Sit down," said Mr Mann kindly. "What do you want me to do for you?"

"I am Mrs Merril," she said timidly.

"So the commissionaire said," replied the little man. "You are nervous about something?"

"Oh, I am so frightened," said the girl, with a shudder. "If he knows I have been here, he'll – "

"You have nothing to be frightened about. Just sit here for one moment."

He went into the next room, which had a branch telephone connection, and called up May. She was out, and he left an urgent message that she was to come, bringing Jasper with her, as soon as she returned. When he got back to his office, he found the girl as he had left her, sitting on the edge of a big armchair, plucking nervously at her handkerchief.

"I have heard about you," she said. "He mentioned you once – before we went to that Sussex cottage with Mr Crawley. They were going to bring another lady and I was to look after her, but he – "

"Who is 'he'?" asked Mr Mann.

"My husband," said the girl.

"How long have you been married?" demanded the little man.

"I ran away with him a long time ago," she said. "It has been an awful life – it was Mr Crawley's idea. He told me that if I married Mr Merril he would take me to see my mother and Jasper. But he was so cruel…"

She shuddered again.

"We've been living in furnished houses all over the country, and I have been alone most of the time and he would not let me go out by myself, or do anything."

She spoke in a subdued, monotonous tone that betrayed the nearness of a bad nervous breakdown.

"What does your husband call himself?"

'Why, Frank Merril," said the girl in astonishment, "that's his name. Mr Crawley always told me his name was Merril. Isn't it?"

Mr Mann shook his head.

"My poor girl," he said sympathetically, "I am afraid you have been grossly deceived. The man you married as Merril is an imposter."

"An imposter?" she faltered.

Mr Mann nodded.

"He has taken a good man's name, and I am afraid has committed abominable crimes in that man's name," said the investigator gently. "I hope we shall be able to rid you and the world of a great villain."

Still she stared uncomprehendingly.

"He has always been a liar," she said slowly. "He lied naturally and acted things so well that you believed him. He told me things which I know aren't true. He told me my brother was dead, and I saw his name in the paper the other day, and that is why I came to you. Do you know Jasper?"

She was as naïve and as unsophisticated as a schoolgirl that it made the little man's heart ache to hear the plaintive monotony of tone and see the trembling lip.

"I promise you that you will meet your brother," he said.

"I have run away from Frank," she said suddenly. "Isn't that a wicked thing to do? I could not stand it. He struck me again yesterday and he pretends to be a gentleman. My mother used to say that no gentleman ever treats a woman badly, but Frank does."

"Nobody shall treat you badly any more," said Mr Mann.

"I hate him," she went on with sudden vehemence. "He sneers and says he's going to get another wife, and – oh!"

He saw her hands go up to her face and saw her staring eyes turn on the door in affright.

Frank Merril stood in the doorway and looked at her without recognition.

"I am sorry," he said. "You have got a visitor."

"Come in," said Mr Mann. "I am awfully glad you called."

The girl had risen to her feet and was shrinking back to the wall.

"Do you know this lady?"

Frank looked at her keenly.

"Why, yes, that's Sergeant Smith's daughter," he said, and he smiled. "Where on earth have you been?"

"Don't touch me," she breathed, and put her hands before her, warding him off.

He looked at her in astonishment and from her to Mann. Then he looked back at the girl, his brow wrinkled in perplexity.

"This girl," said Mr Mann, "thinks she is your wife."

"My wife?" said Frank, and looked again at her. "Is this a bad joke or something – do you say that I am your husband?" he asked.

She did not speak, but nodded slowly.

He sat down in a chair and whistled.

"This rather complicates matters," he said blankly, "but perhaps you can explain?"

"I only know what the girl has told me," said Mr Mann, shaking his head. "I am afraid there is a terrible mistake here."

Frank turned to the girl.

"But did your husband look like me?"

She nodded.

"And did he call himself Frank Merril?"

Again she nodded.

"Where is he now?"

She nodded, this time at him.

"But, great heavens," said Frank, with a gesture of despair, "you do not suggest that *I* am the man?"

"You are the man," said the girl.

Again Frank looked appealingly at his friend, and Saul Arthur Mann saw dismay and laughter in his eyes.

"I don't know what I can do," he said. "Perhaps if you left me alone with her for a minute – "

"Don't, don't," she breathed, "don't leave me alone with him. Stay here."

"And where have you come from now?" asked Frank.

"From the house where you took me. You struck me yesterday," she went on inconsequently.

Frank laughed.

"I am not only married, but I am a wife-beater apparently," he said desperately. "Now what can I do? I think the best thing that can be done is for this lady to tell us where she lives and I will take her back and confront her husband."

"I won't go with you!" cried the girl. "I won't! I won't! – you said you'd look after me, Mr Mann. You promised!"

The little investigator saw that she was distraught to a point where a collapse was imminent.

"This gentleman will look after you also," he said encouragingly. "He is as anxious to save you from your husband as anybody."

"I will not go," she cried. "If that man touches me," and she pointed to Frank, "I'll scream!"

Again came the tap at the door, and Frank looked round.

"More visitors?" he asked.

"It is all right," said Saul Arthur Mann. "There's a lady and a gentleman to see me, isn't there?" he asked the commissionaire. "Show them in, please."

May came first, saw the little tableau and stopped, knowing instinctively all that it portended. Jasper followed her.

The girl, who had been watching Frank, shifted her eyes for a moment to the visitors, and at sight of Jasper flung across the room. In an instant her brother's arms were around her and she was sobbing on his breast.

"I am entitled to ask what all this means?" asked Frank quietly. "I am sure you will overlook my natural irritation, but I have suffered so much and I have been the victim of so many surprises that I do not feel inclined to accept all the shocks which fate sends me in a spirit of joyful resignation. Perhaps you will be good enough to elucidate this new mystery. Is everybody mad – or am I the sole sufferer?"

"There is no mystery about it," said Jasper, still holding the girl. "I think you know this lady?"

"I have never met her before in my life," said Frank, "but she persists in regarding me as her husband, for some reason. Is this a new scheme of yours, Jasper?"

"I think you know this lady," said Jasper Cole again.

Frank shrugged his shoulders.

"You are almost monotonous. I repeat that I have never seen her before."

"Then I will explain to you," said Jasper.

He put the girl gently from him for a moment, and turned and whispered something to May. Together they passed out of the room.

"You were confidential secretary to John Minute for some time, Merril, and in that capacity you made several discoveries. The most remarkable discovery was made when Sergeant Smith came to blackmail my father – oh, don't pretend you didn't know that John Minute was my father," he said, in answer to the look of amazement on Frank Merril's face.

"Smith took you into his confidence and you married his alleged daughter. John Minute discovered this fact, not that he was aware that it was his own daughter or that he thought your association with my sister was any more than an intrigue beneath the dignity of his nephew. You did not think the time was ripe to spring a son-in-law upon him and so you waited until you had seen his will. In that will he made no mention of a daughter, because the child had been born after his wife had left him and he refused to recognise his paternity. Later, in some doubt as to whether he was doing an injustice to what might have been his own child, he endeavoured to find her. Had you known of those investigations, you could have helped considerably; but as it happened, you did not. You married her because you thought you would get a share of John Minute's millions, and when you found your plan had miscarried, you planned an act of bigamy in order to secure a portion of Mr Minute's fortune, which you knew would be considerable."

He turned to Saul Arthur Mann.

"You think I have not been very energetic in pursuing my inquiries as to who killed John Minute? There is the explanation of my tolerance."

He pointed his finger at Frank.

"This man is the husband of my sister. To ruin him would have meant involving her in that ruin. For a time I thought they were happily married. It was only recently that I have discovered the truth."

Frank shook his head.

"I don't know whether to laugh or cry," he said. "I have certainly not heard – "

"You will hear more," said Jasper Cole. "I will tell you how the murder was committed and who was the mysterious Rex Holland.

"Your father was a forger. That is known. You also have been forging signatures since you were a boy. You were Rex Holland. You came to Eastbourne on the night of the murder and by an ingenious device you secured evidence in your favour in advance. Pretending to have lost your ticket, you allowed station officials to search you and to testify that you had no weapon. You were dropped at the gate of my father's house, and, as soon as the cab driver had disappeared, you made your way to where you had hidden your car in a field at a short distance from the house.

"You had arrived there earlier in the evening and you had made your way across the metals to Polegate Junction, where you joined the train. As you had taken the precaution to have your return ticket clipped in London, your trick was not discovered. You had regained your car and drove up to the house ten minutes after you had been seen to disappear through the gateway. From your car you had taken the revolver, and with that revolver you murdered my father. In order to shield yourself, you threw suspicion on me and made friends with one of the shrewdest men" – he inclined his head toward the speechless Mr Mann – "and through him conveyed those suspicions to authoritative quarters. It was you who, having said farewell to Miss Nuttall in Geneva, reappeared the same evening at Montreux and wrote a note forging my handwriting. It was you who left a torn sheet

163

of paper in the room at Number 69 Flowerton Road, also in my writing.

"You have never moved a step but that I have followed you. My agents have been with you day and night ever since the day of the murder. I have waited my time and that has come now."

Frank heaved a long sigh and took up his hat.

"Tomorrow morning I shall have a story to tell," he said.

"You are an excellent actor," said Jasper, "and an excellent liar, but you have never deceived me."

He flung open the door.

"There is your road. You have twenty thousand pounds which my father left you. You have some fifty-five thousand pounds which you buried on the night of the murder – you remember the gardener's trowel in the car?" he said, turning to Mann.

"I give you twenty-four hours to leave England. We cannot try you for the murder of John Minute – you can still be tried for the murder of your unfortunate servants."

Frank Merril made no movement toward the door. He walked over to the other end of the room and stood with his back to them. Then he turned.

"Sometimes," he said, "I feel that it isn't worth while going on. It has been rather a strain – all this."

Jasper Cole sprang toward him and caught him as he fell. They laid him down, and Saul Arthur Mann called urgently on the telephone for a doctor, but Frank Merril was dead.

"I knew," said Constable Wiseman, when the story came to him.

EDGAR WALLACE

BIG FOOT

Footprints and a dead woman bring together Superintendent Minton and the amateur sleuth Mr Cardew. Who is the man in the shrubbery? Who is the singer of the haunting Moorish tune? Why is Hannah Shaw so determined to go to Pawsy, 'a dog lonely place' she had previously detested? Death lurks in the dark and someone must solve the mystery before BIG FOOT strikes again, in a yet more fiendish manner.

BONES IN LONDON

The new Managing Director of Schemes Ltd has an elegant London office and a theatrically dressed assistant – however Bones, as he is better known, is bored. Luckily there is a slump in the shipping market and it is not long before Joe and Fred Pole pay Bones a visit. They are totally unprepared for Bones' unnerving style of doing business, unprepared for his unique style of innocent and endearing mischief.

EDGAR WALLACE

BONES OF THE RIVER

'Taking the little paper from the pigeon's leg, Hamilton saw it was from Sanders and marked URGENT. *Send Bones instantly to Lujamalababa… Arrest and bring to head-quarters the witch doctor.'*

It is a time when the world's most powerful nations are vying for colonial honour, a time of trading steamers and tribal chiefs. In the mysterious African territories administered by Commissioner Sanders, Bones persistently manages to create his own unique style of innocent and endearing mischief.

THE DAFFODIL MYSTERY

When Mr Thomas Lyne, poet, poseur and owner of Lyne's Emporium insults a cashier, Odette Rider, she resigns. Having summoned detective Jack Tarling to investigate another employee, Mr Milburgh, Lyne now changes his plans. Tarling and his Chinese companion refuse to become involved. They pay a visit to Odette's flat. In the hall Tarling meets Sam, convicted felon and protégé of Lyne. Next morning Tarling discovers a body. The hands are crossed on the breast, adorned with a handful of daffodils.

EDGAR WALLACE

THE JOKER

While the millionaire Stratford Harlow is in Princetown, not only does he meet with his lawyer Mr Ellenbury but he gets his first glimpse of the beautiful Aileen Rivers, niece of the actor and convicted felon Arthur Ingle. When Aileen is involved in a car accident on the Thames Embankment, the driver is James Carlton of Scotland Yard. Later that evening Carlton gets a call. It is Aileen. She needs help.

THE SQUARE EMERALD

'Suicide on the left,' says Chief Inspector Coldwell pleasantly, as he and Leslie Maughan stride along the Thames Embankment during a brutally cold night. A gaunt figure is sprawled across the parapet. But Coldwell soon discovers that Peter Dawlish, fresh out of prison for forgery, is not considering suicide but murder. Coldwell suspects Druze as the intended victim. Maughan disagrees. If Druze dies, she says, 'It will be because he does not love children!'

OTHER TITLES BY EDGAR WALLACE AVAILABLE DIRECT
FROM HOUSE OF STRATUS

Quantity		£	$(US)	$(CAN)	€
	THE ADMIRABLE CARFEW	6.99	11.50	15.99	11.50
	THE ANGEL OF TERROR	6.99	11.50	15.99	11.50
	THE AVENGER	6.99	11.50	15.99	11.50
	BARBARA ON HER OWN	6.99	11.50	15.99	11.50
	BIG FOOT	6.99	11.50	15.99	11.50
	THE BLACK ABBOT	6.99	11.50	15.99	11.50
	BONES	6.99	11.50	15.99	11.50
	BONES IN LONDON	6.99	11.50	15.99	11.50
	BONES OF THE RIVER	6.99	11.50	15.99	11.50
	THE CLUE OF THE NEW PIN	6.99	11.50	15.99	11.50
	THE CLUE OF THE SILVER KEY	6.99	11.50	15.99	11.50
	THE CLUE OF THE TWISTED CANDLE	6.99	11.50	15.99	11.50
	THE COAT OF ARMS	6.99	11.50	15.99	11.50
	THE COUNCIL OF JUSTICE	6.99	11.50	15.99	11.50
	THE CRIMSON CIRCLE	6.99	11.50	15.99	11.50
	THE DAFFODIL MYSTERY	6.99	11.50	15.99	11.50
	THE DARK EYES OF LONDON	6.99	11.50	15.99	11.50
	THE DAUGHTERS OF THE NIGHT	6.99	11.50	15.99	11.50
	A DEBT DISCHARGED	6.99	11.50	15.99	11.50
	THE DEVIL MAN	6.99	11.50	15.99	11.50
	THE DOOR WITH SEVEN LOCKS	6.99	11.50	15.99	11.50
	THE DUKE IN THE SUBURBS	6.99	11.50	15.99	11.50
	THE FACE IN THE NIGHT	6.99	11.50	15.99	11.50
	THE FEATHERED SERPENT	6.99	11.50	15.99	11.50
	THE FLYING SQUAD	6.99	11.50	15.99	11.50
	THE FORGER	6.99	11.50	15.99	11.50
	THE FOUR JUST MEN	6.99	11.50	15.99	11.50
	FOUR SQUARE JANE	6.99	11.50	15.99	11.50

ALL HOUSE OF STRATUS BOOKS ARE AVAILABLE FROM GOOD BOOKSHOPS
OR DIRECT FROM THE PUBLISHER:

Internet: www.houseofstratus.com including author interviews, reviews, features.

Email: sales@houseofstratus.com please quote author, title and credit card details.

OTHER TITLES BY EDGAR WALLACE AVAILABLE DIRECT
FROM HOUSE OF STRATUS

Quantity		£	$(US)	$(CAN)	€
	THE FOURTH PLAGUE	6.99	11.50	15.99	11.50
	THE FRIGHTENED LADY	6.99	11.50	15.99	11.50
	GOOD EVANS	6.99	11.50	15.99	11.50
	THE HAND OF POWER	6.99	11.50	15.99	11.50
	THE IRON GRIP	6.99	11.50	15.99	11.50
	THE JOKER	6.99	11.50	15.99	11.50
	THE JUST MEN OF CORDOVA	6.99	11.50	15.99	11.50
	THE KEEPERS OF THE KING'S PEACE	6.99	11.50	15.99	11.50
	THE LAW OF THE FOUR JUST MEN	6.99	11.50	15.99	11.50
	THE LONE HOUSE MYSTERY	6.99	11.50	15.99	11.50
	THE MAN WHO BOUGHT LONDON	6.99	11.50	15.99	11.50
	THE MAN WHO WAS NOBODY	6.99	11.50	15.99	11.50
	THE MIND OF MR J G REEDER	6.99	11.50	15.99	11.50
	MORE EDUCATED EVANS	6.99	11.50	15.99	11.50
	MR J G REEDER RETURNS	6.99	11.50	15.99	11.50
	MR JUSTICE MAXWELL	6.99	11.50	15.99	11.50
	RED ACES	6.99	11.50	15.99	11.50
	ROOM 13	6.99	11.50	15.99	11.50
	SANDERS	6.99	11.50	15.99	11.50
	SANDERS OF THE RIVER	6.99	11.50	15.99	11.50
	THE SINISTER MAN	6.99	11.50	15.99	11.50
	THE SQUARE EMERALD	6.99	11.50	15.99	11.50
	THE THREE JUST MEN	6.99	11.50	15.99	11.50
	THE THREE OAK MYSTERY	6.99	11.50	15.99	11.50
	THE TRAITOR'S GATE	6.99	11.50	15.99	11.50
	WHEN THE GANGS CAME TO LONDON	6.99	11.50	15.99	11.50
	WHEN THE WORLD STOPPED	6.99	11.50	15.99	11.50

Hotline: UK ONLY: **0800 169 1780**, please quote author, title and credit card details.
INTERNATIONAL: **+44 (0) 20 7494 6400**, please quote author, title and credit card details.

Send to: **House of Stratus Sales Department**
24c Old Burlington Street
London
W1X 1RL
UK

Please allow for postage costs charged per order plus an amount per book as set out in the tables below:

	£(Sterling)	$(US)	$(CAN)	€(Euros)
Cost per order				
UK	2.00	3.00	4.50	3.30
Europe	3.00	4.50	6.75	5.00
North America	3.00	4.50	6.75	5.00
Rest of World	3.00	4.50	6.75	5.00
Additional cost per book				
UK	0.50	0.75	1.15	0.85
Europe	1.00	1.50	2.30	1.70
North America	2.00	3.00	4.60	3.40
Rest of World	2.50	3.75	5.75	4.25

PLEASE SEND CHEQUE, POSTAL ORDER (STERLING ONLY), EUROCHEQUE, OR INTERNATIONAL MONEY ORDER (PLEASE CIRCLE METHOD OF PAYMENT YOU WISH TO USE)
MAKE PAYABLE TO: STRATUS HOLDINGS plc

Cost of book(s): ———————— Example: 3 x books at £6.99 each: £20.97

Cost of order: ———————— Example: £2.00 (Delivery to UK address)

Additional cost per book: ———— Example: 3 x £0.50: £1.50

Order total including postage: ——— Example: £24.47

Please tick currency you wish to use and add total amount of order:

☐ £ (Sterling)   ☐ $ (US)   ☐ $ (CAN)   ☐ € (EUROS)

VISA, MASTERCARD, SWITCH, AMEX, SOLO, JCB:

☐☐☐☐☐☐☐☐☐☐☐☐☐☐☐☐☐☐☐

Issue number (Switch only):

☐☐☐

Start Date: **Expiry Date:**

☐☐ / ☐☐   ☐☐ / ☐☐

Signature: _____

NAME: _____

ADDRESS: _____

_____

POSTCODE: _____

Please allow 28 days for delivery.

Prices subject to change without notice.
Please tick box if you do not wish to receive any additional information. ☐

House of Stratus publishes many other titles in this genre; please check our website (**www.houseofstratus.com**) for more details.